BACKSTAGE AT
THE HORSE SHOW!

The Saddle Club quietly made their way backstage past the warm-up ring to the double doors of the arena. The program had begun and the first rider was already out on the course.

Carole watched the second rider waiting to go on. She wondered what must be going through the woman's head. She sat absolutely still on her horse. Her face was a study in stony concentration as she took long, deep breaths.

"Thirty seconds," a woman by the door told the rider. The rider only blinked acknowledgment.

There was applause from the audience. Carole could hear the first competitor's horse cantering toward the door. The door swung open to admit them.

"Smile!" the starter told the rider. The rider's entire face changed. All solemnity was gone. Her face became the picture of joy and confidence. She gave her horse an almost invisible signal and the horse sprang to life. Together, they bounded out into the arena, ready for the ride of their lives. It almost took Carole's breath away.

THE SADDLE CLUB

Horse Show

Bonnie Bryant

A BANTAM SKYLARK BOOK®
NEW YORK · TORONTO · LONDON · SYDNEY · AUCKLAND

I would like to express special thanks to Marie C. Lafrenz and Karen Hurley, who helped immensely with horse show lore, to Kathy Fallon of the American Horse Show Association, and to Dr. Peter J. Zeale.

RL 5, 009–012

HORSE SHOW
A Bantam Skylark Book / December 1989

Skylark Books is a registered trademark of Bantam Books,
a division of Bantam Doubleday Dell Publishing Group, Inc.
Registered in U.S. Patent and Trademark Office and elsewhere.

"The Saddle Club" is a trademark of Bonnie
Bryant Hiller. The Saddle Club design/logo, which
consists of an inverted U-shaped design, a riding crop,
and a riding hat, is a trademark of Bantam Books.

ISBN 0-553-15769-8

Published simultaneously in the United States and Canada

Bantam Books are published by Bantam Books, a division of Bantam Doubleday Dell Publishing Group, Inc. Its trademark, consisting of the words
"Bantam Books" and the portrayal of a rooster, is Registered in U.S. Patent
and Trademark Office and in other countries. Marca Registrada. Bantam
Books, 666 Fifth Avenue, New York, New York 10103.

PRINTED IN THE UNITED STATES OF AMERICA

0 9 8 7 6 5 4 3 2 1

—For Suzanne Ziegler

1

Lisa Atwood sat on a bench in the locker area at Pine Hollow Stables and removed one of her boots. She barely noticed what she was doing. Her mind wasn't on boots. It was on horse shows. She'd just learned that Max Regnery, her instructor and the owner of Pine Hollow, was going to the American Horse Show in New York to watch his former student Dorothy DeSoto ride. Lisa had met Dorothy when she had given a small demonstration at Pine Hollow. But the American Horse Show . . . It made Lisa shiver with excitement just to think about it.

Lisa loved horses. She loved riding them and taking care of them. Although she was quite a new rider—she'd been riding for less than a year—Max said she had a lot of potential. She worked hard at her riding, but it was fun work, mostly because she did it with her two best friends. Stevie Lake and Carole Hanson were definitely horse crazy, too.

Lisa pulled off her second boot, stuffed it in her cubby, and began combing her long light brown hair in front of the dim little mirror. She daydreamed about the American Horse Show. She'd seen some horse shows, mostly on television. The American Horse Show was the most important one in the country. She could almost feel the thrill of being there. Max would be there, as well as his mother, Mrs. Reg. Lisa would just be in Willow Creek, Virginia, reading about it in the paper.

"I just heard the most exciting thing!" Stevie bubbled as she bounded into the locker area. "Guess what Max and Mrs. Reg are doing next week? You'll never guess! They're going—"

"Max is going to New York!" Carole announced from the doorway. "Can you believe it? He and his mother are going to the American Horse Show to—"

"See Dorothy DeSoto compete," Lisa said, finishing Carole's sentence for her.

"How did you know?" Carole and Stevie asked her, almost in unison.

"I saw that Max's classes were canceled for next week, so I asked him why," Lisa explained. "How did you find out?"

"I did the same thing," Carole said.

"And so did I," Stevie said, plopping down on the

bench, next to Lisa. "Max must be wondering if we three ever talk to one another!"

"He knows we talk to one another," Lisa said sensibly. "He knows it because we're *always* doing it in class—and he doesn't like that!" she added, giggling.

"Well, I think we're going to have to do some more talking," Carole said. She sounded very serious. Her tone made Lisa look away from the mirror. "So let's have a Saddle Club meeting at TD's in . . ." She looked at her watch. "How 'bout one half hour."

That sounded like a good idea to Lisa and Stevie. There was always time for a sundae at the Tastee Delight ice cream store. A half an hour gave them just enough time to change their clothes and get to the meeting on time.

The Saddle Club was a group the girls had formed. The three of them were the only active members, though there was one out-of-state friend who was an honorary member. The requirements for membership were that each girl had to be horse crazy (which they all were) and had to help other members when they were in trouble (which they did). Trouble could include horseback riding, but it could also mean schoolwork, family problems, or, occasionally, boy trouble. When friends needed help, Saddle Club girls were there.

The Saddle Club didn't have formally scheduled meetings. The girls just got together when it seemed like a good idea. Most of the time, Saddle Club meetings meant gossiping about horses and riding. This time, Lisa suspected Carole had something more specific on her mind.

The girls usually met at TD's. It was at the local shopping center, home of a supermarket, an electronics shop, a jewelry store, and a couple of shoe stores. Other shops there came and went at a rapid clip. Fortunately for The Saddle Club, TD's stayed in business. It was the girls' favorite hangout.

"Isn't it exciting!" Carole said, after they had given the waitress their orders. It was almost exactly a half hour later, and they were sitting in their favorite back booth at TD's. "Max is going to New York!"

"What's so exciting about that?" Stevie asked, trying to sound very cool. "I went to New York with my family last year. We saw a lot of dirt and garbage, some tall buildings, and an island full of people in a rush."

"But you didn't see the American Horse Show, did you?" Carole asked.

"Nope. We did see the Rockettes at Radio City Music Hall. Does that count?"

"No, it definitely does not count," Carole told her. When Carole's mind was on horses, that was all she wanted to talk about. "There's no comparison between show girls in sequinned costumes doing high kicks and a *real* horse show."

4

"I bet my brother Chad would disagree," Stevie joked.

When Carole got too single-minded, Stevie took it as a personal mission to try to loosen her up. It was a way she had of teasing Carole.

"I got a new issue of *Teen Month*," Stevie said to Lisa. "They've got a whole article on Skye Ransom. He's making a new movie and it's called *City Cowboy*. He is *so* cute!"

"You can say that again," Lisa said, sighing dreamily.

Stevie giggled. "He's so cu—"

"Can we stick to the subject?" Carole asked.

"We are sticking to it," Stevie said. "See, in this movie, Skye has to ride a horse. Wait'll you see the picture of him in breeches and boots. He's just—"

"I bet he's a wonderful rider," Lisa said. She thought Skye Ransom was just plain wonderful. "He does *everything*. Remember in his last movie when he had to do all that dancing? And the one before when he was playing the guitar?"

"I heard that somebody else actually played the music," Stevie said.

"Well, he *looked* like he did it well and that's what's important in a movie," Lisa said. She didn't mind making allowances for someone as cute as Skye Ransom. "You know what I heard? I heard that *City Cowboy*, Skye's new movie, is being filmed in New York. Maybe Max will see him when he's in New York!"

5

"I doubt it," Stevie said, "but you never know."

"Ahem," Carole said. "And that brings us back to the subject—which was the American Horse Show in New York next week," she said, reminding her friends why they were there. "When Skye Ransom can compete in the American, we can talk about him at a Saddle Club meeting."

"Horse show?" Stevie said innocently. "You mean the American Horse Show, where Max and Mrs. Reg are going to watch Dorothy DeSoto compete? The one we wish we could go to?"

"That's *just* it!" Carole said, obviously relieved that the conversation had finally gotten to where she wanted it. "We wish we could go, too."

"Wouldn't it be fantastic?" Stevie said. She was done teasing Carole, and her attention was now turned completely to the horse show. "The American isn't like any other horse show. It's the real thing. The big one. The best riders in the world will be there. Including Dorothy DeSoto." She sighed. "Maybe if we begged our parents they would let us go," she said.

"I don't know about you, but I'm not the begging type," Lisa said, a bit primly. Lisa was, in fact, always sensible and logical and organized. As she scraped hot fudge from the side of her dish she thought about what it would mean to be able to go to the American Horse Show and to see the greatest riders in the world. She could feel the excitement of the competition. She began to imagine what she would learn from watching those riders. She realized it would be helpful to her. And exciting, too. "So maybe I should threaten to lie down on the train tracks in front of an oncoming train," she suggested.

Stevie giggled. "I could just about see you do that—the same day I offer to wash dishes for a month to get my parents to let me go or, even worse, promise to keep my room clean!"

"I think I'd promise Dad I'd polish all his brass for the next inspection," Carole said. Her father, a colonel in the Marine Corps, had to keep his brass shinier than all the troops. "Even the buttons on his dress uniform. And I'd promise to remember every single homework assignment all year long, too."

"If they won't go for the train-tracks bit, maybe my mother would let me go if I promised her I'd take up ballet, piano, violin, painting, and needlework lessons again," Lisa said.

"You really used to take all that stuff?" Stevie asked with a groan.

Lisa nodded. "My mother has a lot of ideas about what makes a 'proper young lady.' Unfortunately, they don't include most of the things that interest me."

"You're more proper than I am," Stevie said.

"Almost anybody's more proper than you are," Lisa teased, knowing Stevie would agree with her. She did.

"I think Stevie should talk to Max," Carole said, suddenly serious. She turned to Stevie. "I don't know how you manage to talk him into things, but you do have a track record, so you're appointed." She turned to Lisa. "And everybody knows you're totally sensible. You are an expert at convincing parents—"

"Everyone's but mine," Lisa cut in.

"I was about to get to that," Carole said, continuing. Her dark brown eyes gleamed with excitement. "You talk to my father and to Stevie's parents. You talk them into letting *us* go, then Stevie can talk your parents into letting you go."

Lisa could see the logic of Carole's plan. If she could convince Carole's dad and Stevie's parents, it would be a breeze to convince her own. Maybe.

Inspired with the idea of pulling off the Great Convincing Plan, as the girls called it, they plotted busily while they finished their ice-cream sundaes.

Stevie tried to rehearse her speech to Max. "Why Max!" she cooed. "Wouldn't it be much easier for you and Mrs. Reg in New York if you had the three of us along to run errands for you?"

Carole rolled her eyes to the ceiling. "Give me a break," she said. "What kind of errands are we going to run for them?"

Stevie wrinkled her nose in thought. "We could buy them some subway tokens," she suggested. "You need a lot of them in New York. Or, we could flag taxis for them. I bet Mrs. Reg will like taking taxis."

"Maybe, but I don't think that's the way to convince Max. Why don't you try something about how good it will be for our riding experience to see the champions."

"Right!" Lisa chimed in enthusiastically. "And how great it will be to see Dorothy ride again. She'll be on Topside, won't she?"

Topside was Dorothy DeSoto's championship horse and her favorite. "That pair has won more blue ribbons together than most people could even imagine. I bet she has a whole room full of ribbons in her house."

"*I* bet she has a whole *house* full of ribbons," Stevie said. "Wouldn't it be great if we could actually go?"

The Saddle Club meeting continued. The girls switched back and forth between topics, but they always returned to the main subject: how much they wanted to go to New York. They didn't notice when the waitress at TD's gave them a look to hurry up. They didn't notice when school friends of theirs came in. They didn't even notice the time, until it was very late.

"Yipes!" Lisa exclaimed, finally looking at her wristwatch. "My mother was expecting me home hours ago. If I know her, she's called out the state police by now!"

"No way," Stevie said with a grin. "The first place they would check is here!"

"This is no joke," Lisa said. "After all, I'm supposed to do some heavy convincing and it's not going to be easy if I'm in the doghouse. I'd better give her a call."

9

She stood up from the table and rushed to the pay phone. Then she hurriedly dropped the coins in and dialed her home number. She was only a few minutes away, but her mother was a born worrier. Lisa had recently realized that there was no way she could keep her mother from worrying. It was easier just to keep from giving her anything to worry about.

"Hi, Mom, it's me," she said.

"Oh, I'm so glad you called!" her mother said. "You really have to hurry home, Lisa. I mean, get here right away!"

There was such urgency in her mother's voice that it concerned Lisa.

"What's up, Mom?" she asked, feeling her stomach begin to churn.

"Well, it's Max," her mother said. "He called a while ago. Said he wanted you and your friends to go on a trip to New York with him. Something about a student of his and some little horse show? Anyway, you must get home right away. We have to look over all of your clothes. You don't have a thing to wear in New York!"

At first, Lisa could not believe her ears. Then she almost could not keep from laughing. While she and her friends had been working out the most devious plot in the world to solve what seemed like an insurmountable problem, Max had solved it for them!

"I'll be there right away," Lisa assured her mother. "Sorry I was so late to call you."

"Oh, that's all right, dear," her mother said cheerfully. When she had a project like outfitting Lisa for a trip to New York, Mrs. Atwood could be downright easygoing.

Walking on air, Lisa returned to her friends.

"I can't believe it!" she announced, pulling out her chair.

"What's the big deal?" Stevie asked. "Was your Mom mad?"

"It's so amazing . . ."

"*What?*" Carole asked.

"You'll never guess—"

"Tell us," Stevie demanded.

Lisa clasped her hands in front of her, her eyes sparkling. She couldn't hold it in any longer. "We're going to New York!" she squealed.

"I THINK I forgot my hairbrush," Carole said one week later as the three girls sat on a train bound for New York City. They were on the Metroliner, and the New Jersey countryside rushed past them.

"You didn't forget it," Lisa said, glancing at Stevie and rolling her eyes. "You just used it fifteen minutes ago. It's in your purse."

"Oh, right," Carole said, checking the contents of her overstuffed bag. "Yeah, and here are my slippers, too."

Stevie started giggling. Carole, who never forgot anything having to do with horses, could be very disorganized about everything else. Her packing showed it.

"Well, I think I forgot my boot hooks," Lisa remarked.

"You can't have forgotten anything," Stevie said. "You brought four suitcases!" Stevie recalled how both of Lisa's parents had helped her carry the bags from the car to the train station. She was pretty sure she'd have to help with Lisa's bags when they got to Penn Station in New York. She just hoped they weren't *too* heavy.

"Not me," Lisa told her. "My mother packed them. I have no idea what she put in there, but I bet she didn't remember the boot hooks."

"You can use mine when we go riding—*if* we go riding," Carole said.

"How can it be so hard to go riding in such a wonderful place as New York?" Stevie said. Max had told the girls that there was only one riding stable near them in the city. She couldn't believe that was true, though. New York was so big!

"New York City, Pennsylvania Station in ten minutes!" the conductor announced.

"Pennsylvania Station *and* Madison Square Garden, site of the American Horse Show," Carole said, as if to correct the conductor.

"New York's the site of a lot more than that," Lisa reminded Carole. "There's Greenwich Village, the Empire State Building, Broadway and Times Square, the Statue of Liberty—have I forgotten anything?" she asked.

"Yeah, how about Bloomingdales, Lord & Taylor, Bergdorf Goodman, Tiffany's, and Saks Fifth Avenue?" Stevie joked.

"A little out of my price range," Lisa said.

"Well then, how about all the great shops in

Greenwich Village? I read about this barbershop there where we can get our hair dyed purple."

"Just the exact color my mother's face would be if I ever did that!" Lisa joked.

Max and Mrs. Reg came over then and told the girls to collect their belongings and not to forget anything on the train. Stevie smiled to herself. Those were exactly the same things her parents would have said to her if they'd been there. Her mother had been a little concerned about her being homesick. How could she be homesick when it seemed as if her parents were still with her?

The train ducked into a dark tunnel, passing under the Hudson River and carrying them into Manhattan, the heart of New York City. Stevie didn't like to admit how excited she was, even to herself—but she knew that she was so excited that she'd even help Lisa carry her bags!

In the end, she did help Lisa. So did Carole and so did Max. Lisa kept apologizing, but everybody understood. It was her mother who had packed. Stevie and Carole were content with a couple of pairs of jeans and a few shirts, a dress, just in case, and riding clothes. Lisa would have been, too, but not her mother.

"I think I've got the one with the bricks in it." Stevie gave an exaggerated moan as she hefted the suitcase up the ramp into Penn Station.

"You got bricks, I got dumbbells," Carole announced.

"I'm sorry, you guys!" Lisa grimaced and grunted. "And I got the rock collection!"

Fortunately, they didn't have to carry anything far. Madison Square Garden, it turned out, was in a building that sort of sat on Penn Station. Max had them stow all their bags in lockers in the station so they could go straight upstairs to the horse show.

Max showed the guard at the show their passes and got directions to find Dorothy.

Madison Square Garden was not a garden at all. The only flowers Stevie saw were fake. But it was a big building and a busy one. Max led the way up escalators and along hallways. Stevie had been expecting masses of crowds, but it was early afternoon on the day before the show and, according to the program she'd gotten on the way in, it was a practice session. There were just small crowd noises coming down the ramps from the arena.

"Max, can we look?" Carole asked, pointing toward the source of the noises.

Max smiled. "Oh, sure." He understood their curiosity about everything.

Carole walked through the short hallway. Lisa and Stevie followed. At first, all Stevie could see were seats up above, and then the spotlights from the ceiling. Then, with one more upward step, there was Madison Square Garden and there was the American Horse Show!

The Garden seemed enormous. It was an oval

arena, perhaps half the size of a football field, with rows and rows of seats surrounding it. The arena was covered now with soft dirt, but Stevie knew she'd watched televised tennis and basketball and ice-hockey games from the same place, too. She was amazed to think what was involved in the transformation from a riding ring to a basketball court to a hockey rink.

"Imagine this place with a basketball game in it," she said to Carole.

"Don't be silly," Carole said. "The ball would never bounce properly on the dirt."

That, Stevie thought to herself, was a good example of Carole being so focused on horses that she was flaky. She knew there was no point in saying anything to Carole. That's just the way she was. Stevie smiled to herself and followed the group to the backstage area.

They walked along twisty hallways, past doors that said things like Rangers Locker Room. No Entry. The Rangers was the hockey team that played there.

Two more lefts, a right, and then another left, and the smell was unmistakable. They were backstage at the horse show.

They had to climb over some trailers that had jumps stored on them. They walked around two tractors and circled a couple of pillars. Then they were there.

The first thing they noticed was a small area where the concrete floor was covered with a foot or more of dirt. Three riders were cantering their horses in circles in a space little bigger than a junior-high-school class-room. It was obviously the warm-up area, but Carole thought it must be hard to warm up in such a confined space. Beyond the warm-up ring was a large area turned into temporary stables. Endless rows of metal fences had been set up to make four- by eight-foot stalls for the championship horses who were compet-ing in the show. The owners who were bringing several horses had hung their stables' colors on the fences to identify themselves. Tack hung outside the small stalls or was stowed in trunks for each horse.

Carole couldn't decide whether it was wonderful or awful. On the wonderful side, she'd never seen so many absolutely beautiful horses in one place at the same time. There were perhaps a hundred horses there. On the awful side, it seemed to her that there was nowhere near enough room in that place for a hundred horses! Each one of the animals deserved at least twice as much space. Horses without room to move about could become very restless.

Max paused to check the floor plan so he'd know where Dorothy was. Carole took the opportunity to check out one of the champions.

According to his nameplate, his name was Wor-cestershire—"Probably because he's so saucy," Stevie whispered. Carole giggled. He was a Thoroughbred gelding, a chestnut like the horse Stevie usually rode. His coat gleamed. His eyes were bright and his ears twitched at all the noises around him, but he did not seem nervous at all. In fact, he munched contentedly on some hay in his manger. Carole thought he looked as if he'd been through the entire routine before. He'd be ready when it was time to perform, but until then, he'd just stay cool.

"This way," Max announced, pointing down one of the aisles of stalls. The group began moving again, stepping carefully around trunks, over buckets, under tack and drying blankets, and through puddles.

"Dorothy!" Max called out.

Halfway down the aisle, Dorothy DeSoto was crouched in front of her horse, Topside, polishing his hooves. She set down her brush and hurried to greet her guests. Max gave her a big hug. So did Mrs. Reg. The Saddle Club girls were not sure what to do. Dorothy made it easy; she hugged them!

"I'm so glad you came!" she said. "You put on such a great show for me when I was in Willow Creek that I just knew you had to come to this one!"

"Oh, wow," Carole said. Her friends had the feeling that at that instant Carole was so starstruck that she really was not capable of saying anything else.

"Can I say hello to Topside?" Lisa asked.

"Be my guest," Dorothy said. The three girls all went over to the horse. Topside was a bay, meaning his coat was brown and his points—mane, tail, nose, and ankles—were black. It was a common color pattern, but didn't make Topside any less special.

The groom working on Topside's coat stood up. "You still teach your students how to do work, Max, or are you mollycoddling them these days?" the groom asked.

"Girls, meet my mother, Jean," Dorothy said. The Saddle Club looked at the woman, a little stunned.

"My students are as lazy as they always were. Never can get enough experienced help," Max teased. "This trio, particularly, needs experience. You want them to finish grooming Topside?"

Max had barely finished his sentence before Stevie, Lisa, and Carole were reaching for the grooming equipment. Stevie and Lisa worked on Topside's coat. Carole picked up the brush to finish polishing his hooves.

Max invited Dorothy and Mrs. DeSoto to join him and Mrs. Reg for coffee.

"I'm riding at about two-thirty," Dorothy told the girls. "It's a practice session, and I've got the ring all to myself for ten minutes. You can watch if you'd like."

"We sure would," Carole said enthusiastically, speaking for all of them. "And don't worry. Topside will be shipshape before you go out in the ring, Dorothy."

"I know," Dorothy said. "See, I know who trained you!" She gave Max's arm a squeeze and the four adults left for the coffee shop.

Topside glanced over his shoulder and regarded Stevie dubiously. She patted him to reassure him. He looked over his other shoulder at Lisa.

"Checking out the new beauty-parlor crew?" Lisa asked him. "Don't worry. We know what we're doing."

She put the comb to his coat and drew it along his shiny flank. He seemed to accept her manner so he turned his attention to Carole.

"Ah, now you want to meet the new manicurist?" Carole said with a smile, putting the finishing touches on the polish on his left rear hoof. She then turned her attention to his right front one, using a hoof-pick to remove the accumulated dirt.

Having approved the work crew, Topside relaxed and enjoyed all the attention. The girls had studied all aspects of grooming with Max and they really did know what they were doing. Topside sensed that. He whinnied contentedly.

Stevie felt incredibly lucky to be grooming a horse as great as Topside. He was a true champion. Of course, much of the credit went to Dorothy, Stevie knew. But a good horse would make the difference between winning and losing, no matter how good the rider. As she polished his coat, she dreamed about what it would be like to ride him someday. She could imagine the powerful animal under her command, instantly following every signal she gave him. She looked at his strong legs and beautifully taut body and thought what it would feel like to jump over a fence on Topside. With strength like his, it would be smooth as glass, she imagined—like flying!

"I said, are you finished or are you going to rub a

bare spot on his flank with the towel?" Carole asked, interrupting Stevie's daydream.

"Oh, sorry," Stevie said, a little embarrassed. "I just got to thinking about what a wonderful horse he is. He's just beautiful. Can you imagine riding him?"

Carole smiled knowingly. "Yes, I can. Listen, Dorothy's turn in the ring is in an hour and a half. Let's take a look around until she gets back with Max and Mrs. Reg."

The girls wandered throughout the stabling area and then watched the riders warm up their horses in the ring. They found that the little ring was near the main door to the arena. A big set of double doors by the warm-up ring opened onto the arena. Cautiously, the girls edged toward it. Nobody stopped them. The badges they wore seemed to work magic. They walked through the doors and into the arena. Workmen in coveralls were everywhere, attaching red-white-and-blue bunting around the edge, setting up jumps for the practice session, and moving seats. An electronic scoreboard flashed meaningless numbers to test the system. Above them, in a special booth, an announcer tried out the public-address system. He seemed to be practicing saying the names of all the riders and their horses so he would not make any mistakes when the show started the next day.

Then, faster than the girls would have thought possible, the jumps were set up and the practice session began.

It was helpful to horses and riders to have a time like that in the arena before the competition began. It gave the riders a chance to exercise their horses in an open space. It was an hour until Dorothy's appearance so the girls settled into some of the red seats in Madison Square Garden and watched. They couldn't get enough of it. It was so exciting to watch the work that went behind championship competition.

The first rider out was a man on a very tall gray mare. He trotted his horse around the ring to familiarize her with it and then they cantered. The girls could almost feel the horse relaxing as she became comfortable with her surroundings. The rider then spent most of the rest of the time approaching the first jump and going over it.

"The first jump will be someplace else in the actual competition," Carole explained to her friends. "The jump course is always different. The idea, though, is that if he can calm her down and get her to concentrate on the first jump, she'll be better at the rest of them."

Then the announcer told the rider that his ten minutes were up. The rider hurried the mare back to the stable area, and the next rider came out. This time, it was a woman, riding a bay gelding. The horse was very frisky, bucking and bouncing all over the place. It seemed like the horse was out of control.

"Don't pay any attention to the style here," Carole said. "This particular event—the jumpers—is one of speed and accuracy. The horses have to get over all the jumps as fast as possible. It doesn't matter what they look like when they do it. A frisky horse like this can really make time, too. Just wait and see."

Stevie grinned to herself. Having a friend like Carole was better than an encyclopedia sometimes! Carole went on to explain that there was another type of jumping called hunter jumping in which the things that mattered most were style and manners.

Stevie watched the bay gelding. Fussy as he was, he negotiated the practice course much faster than the gray mare. Still, this was a practice session and there was no telling what would happen at the real thing.

The girls watched a few more horses and then returned to Topside's stall to help Dorothy tack up in time for her session. They found she'd already gotten all the tack on and was in the warm-up ring a half hour before her call.

"Topside needs a long exercise period before he goes out into the ring," Jean DeSoto explained to the girls. "Dorothy's always found it works best for him, even when it's just a practice session. See, at our farm on Long Island, he has the freedom of a stall and a small paddock to himself. It's bad for him to be cooped up in that little stall, and the only way around it is to let him work out the kinks in this little warm-up ring."

The girls stood by and watched. They could see Topside ease up as Dorothy rode him in circles. He became more responsive to her signals and more supple as the time passed.

"I think he's ready," Dorothy said.

"He looks good," Max told her.

"Dorothy DeSoto!" the backstage speakers blared out. "Two minutes!"

Dorothy cantered Topside around the ring two more times, then walked him to settle him. Then the doors opened, a horse and rider trotted in, and Dorothy and Topside walked out.

The girls and Max slipped into ringside seats to watch.

As with the other riders the girls had watched, Dorothy rode Topside around the arena until it was familiar to him, then she began the practice work.

Carefully and methodically, Dorothy led Topside through a routine that was obviously familiar to them. They seemed relaxed, and worked together in perfect unison. Stevie held her breath as they sailed over the jumps. She could almost feel the wind brushing her own cheeks, the thrill of each effortless takeoff and landing. Stevie was sure they'd only begun their practice when she heard the announcer say, "Time, Ms. DeSoto."

Obediently, Dorothy returned backstage. The girls helped her untack Topside, gave him another grooming, a bit of water, and some fresh hay and straw for bedding.

"The show begins tomorrow," Dorothy said. "But my first event isn't until the day after. That gives us the rest of today and all of tomorrow to give you girls a taste of the Big Apple."

Stevie could barely believe that there could be something more exciting coming up for them than what they'd already seen. Seeing things in New York would be okay, she thought, but probably not as good as being backstage at the American Horse Show!

LISA TOOK THE last of her suitcases out of the trunk of the taxicab, which had stopped in front of Dorothy's house. She gratefully accepted when Stevie and Max each offered to help carry the four bags inside. She carried two bags herself.

"Next time, I'm doing my own packing!" she vowed.

Max hefted one of her bags. His grimace told her he thought that was a very good idea.

Dorothy's house was a four-story private house. It reminded Lisa of the houses she'd seen in Washington's Georgetown. It was red brick with white-trimmed windows. On either side, right next to it, were other identical houses. A lot of the other houses on the street were similar, but at the end of the block, there was a tall apartment building. It looked strange next to the little houses.

"This neighborhood is called Greenwich Village," Dorothy told the girls. "It's an odd mix of old, historic houses, like this one, and new buildings. The streets are crooked and don't make much sense, but you get used to them. Most of the streets probably follow old cow paths. See, this area used to be a summer place for city residents, back when the city was what we now call the Financial District, or Wall Street. Then, there was a typhoid epidemic. A lot of the healthy residents of the city fled to their summer homes to escape the disease. People who didn't have houses here came anyway and built temporary homes as fast as they could. So much for city planning. The temporary homes ended up defining permanent streets. So, we have things like the corner where Waverly Place crosses itself."

"I'm going to love this place," Stevie said, grinning at her friends.

"Yes, you are," Dorothy assured her. "You girls are sharing a room on the third floor. Why don't you take your bags up and unpack, though I doubt there's enough closet space for all your duds, Lisa," she teased. Lisa blushed, annoyed at her mother all over again. "Then come on down and I'll give you a map so you can explore."

Dorothy didn't have to say that twice. The girls grabbed their bags and hurried up the two flights to their room.

The room was bright and sunny. The two windows

looked onto a small yard with a red-brick fence around it. There was a fruit tree there and some flowers and bushes. It wasn't the rolling hills of Virginia, but it was pretty in a citified way. Lisa rather liked it.

Stevie and Carole joined her at the window. "Not much to mow, is there?" Carole remarked.

"No, and no room for a swimming pool, either," Stevie added.

"But it's nice, you know," Lisa said. "It's sort of like, in New York, a little garden like this is so precious that you have to make the best of it."

"And I thought everybody in the city lived in cramped apartments," Carole said.

"From what I heard," Stevie said, "I thought everyone *in* the city lived *out of* the city!"

"That's what I thought, but I don't think I'd mind it if I lived in a house like this," Lisa said. She was surprised at herself. She had never thought about living in a city because she had always lived in the country. It made her very curious to learn more about the city and the neighborhood. "Let's finish unpacking and get exploring!" she said.

"Great idea, if you've got about three hours to unload your suitcases!"

Lisa considered the size of the task and made up her mind. "All right, let's explore and *never* unpack!"

The girls hurried downstairs.

They found Max and Dorothy having a heated discussion, almost an argument, about whether the girls could go out into the city by themselves.

"I'll give them a map, Max. They can find their way around the neighborhood by themselves."

"But their parents!" Max protested. "I promised them the girls would be safe!"

"They will be," Dorothy said calmly. "It's broad daylight. It's a warm afternoon and the streets will be filled with pedestrians."

"Or muggers," Max said darkly.

"No self-respecting mugger is going to take a wallet from a thirteen-year-old girl. They know from experience that all they'll get is a couple of dollars and a picture of Tom Cruise clipped from *Teen Month*."

"Skye Ransom," Stevie corrected her. "Tom Cruise is too old."

Max and Dorothy looked at her in surprise and then burst into laughter. Max shook his head. "You win," he said to Dorothy. "Give them the map. Give them your phone number. Out they go!"

"Don't worry, Max," Lisa reassured in her straight-A-student voice. "After all, we're country girls. We're used to following cow paths. Greenwich Village will be a breeze."

"Okay, already." Max relented totally.

It took a few more minutes for Dorothy to arm them with everything they needed. She highlighted streets on the map where they could find quaint houses, and then she marked where the best shopping would be for them and showed them where they'd find the city's famous Washington Square Park. Dorothy was obviously a history buff, as well as a championship rider, and she told them more interesting things about the development of the neighborhood.

"This whole section, where you'll find the fun stores, is in the heart of a big university. It's a really fun area, so enjoy yourselves."

"And don't talk to strangers, don't buy anything that's not from a store. Don't cross streets against the light. Always have a quarter handy for a phone call. Keep your money carefully put away at the bottom of your purses. And stay together," Max said. He paused to take a breath.

Lisa thought he was about to add to his list of warnings, but Dorothy cut him off. "What he means is use your common sense, girls."

That was something they could understand.

It took them exactly three minutes to get lost. They left Dorothy's, went to the corner of her block, turned right, and then turned left at the next corner.

Lisa consulted the map. "We're supposed to be here," she said, but when she looked at the street signs, they were nowhere near "here."

"I don't care," Stevie said boldly. She peered around a corner. "Look, there's a fun-looking shop. Let's go see what they've got."

It *was* a fun shop. It had a great selection of sweaters, all of which the girls liked and none of which they could afford.

"Look at this gorgeous turtleneck," Lisa said, picking up a heather-colored angora. "I wish I could get it."

"That's all she needs," Stevie said. "Something else to pack!"

"Come on," Carole told her friends. "Let's get moving. We've got so much to see."

"If only we knew where we were," Lisa said.

"It doesn't matter where we are. When the time comes, we'll figure it out and get back. For now, let's go!" Stevie said, cheering on her friends.

The rule when they were riding horses was that the person in the lead was in charge. They followed the same principle adventuring in New York. Lisa was glad Stevie was in the lead. If she'd been in charge herself, she would have insisted on following the map, and it turned out to be much more fun to wander.

"Check that out!" Carole said, her jaw dropping open.

Lisa looked in the direction Carole was pointing. There, coming toward them, was a man with short cropped blond hair—at least most of it was blond. The longer part along the top of his head, Mohawk style, was actually a bright pink.

"Nice," Stevie said. "See how the pink perfectly matches the feathers in his earrings!"

Lisa snorted with laughter. The man was close

enough to hear, but he did not appear to notice the girls gaping at him.

"I wonder how he did it!" Carole said.

"I think it's the kind of thing you have to get done," Lisa said. "After all, nobody's best friend would do that for them, would they?"

"Worst enemy, maybe," Stevie suggested. "Do you suppose he actually paid money to have that done?"

"Yeah, and here comes another one, too," Carole said.

The girls stopped walking and looked. This time the hairdo was on a woman. She probably actually had a lot of hair, but it had been moussed flat against her head on the sides. At the top, it stood straight on end, from ear to ear, and had been fashioned into large green spikes.

"And I thought we had to take a boat to get to the Statue of Liberty!" Stevie said. The girls giggled to themselves.

This time, the subject of their laughter did notice the attention. "Like it?" she asked.

"It's interesting," Stevie offered.

"Well, there's this place," the woman said. "It's right around the corner. They'll do anything you can describe. I couldn't make up my mind between this and a sort of rainbow look, you know? Think I made the right choice?"

Even Stevie could not think of anything to say to that. The girls just nodded.

"We've got to see this place," Carole said. The girls followed directions and found themselves standing in front of a large barbershop filled with customers.

"There must be a hundred people in there!" Lisa noted. "Are they all getting colored spikes?"

"I dare you," Stevie said to Lisa.

Tentatively, Lisa felt her long hair. She could use a cut. She didn't think spikes were a really good idea.

"I double-dare you," Carole said. "Your hair's getting shaggy. You *do* need a cut."

There was something about being alone with her friends in New York City that gave Lisa a surge of energy. She didn't really feel like straight-A-student Lisa Atwood, quiet little junior-high-school girl of Willow Creek, Virginia. She felt positively daring.

"Okay," she said. "Wait for me here."

Leaving two astonished friends outside the barbershop, Lisa entered. Although there had been some weird hairdos coming out, there were plenty of normal-looking customers emerging, too. Lisa was determined to be one of them.

"Just a regular cut," she told the woman sitting on a ladder inside the shop. The woman directed her to an operator named Joyce at the back of the large room.

It only took a few minutes. Lisa had never had her hair cut so fast in her life. And Joyce was good, too. First she trimmed Lisa's long hair to about shoulder length. She also cut one side at a slight angle, longer in the front than in the back. "The wavy bob is really popular," the woman told her. It made Lisa look mature and worldly and that was exactly the way Lisa was feeling that day.

Feeling very grown up, she paid for the cut, gave Joyce a tip, and emerged from the shop.

"Cool!" Stevie said enviously. Carole nodded agreement. Lisa smiled happily. There was a whole new her emerging in the magic of the city.

"If my watch is right, it's time to head back toward Dorothy's, so we'd better get unlost now," Lisa said. She pulled out the map and did some serious work.

It took a few minutes to locate themselves. They stopped six people to ask where they were. Two did not speak English. Three were from out of town. The sixth showed them that they only had to cross the park and walk a couple of blocks to get to Dorothy's. It seemed like a long walk, but they set off.

The park turned out to be the one Dorothy had talked about, Washington Square Park. As soon as the girls saw it, they recognized the arch from movies and television shows about the city.

"We've got to check this out!" Stevie said, leading the way. It was a warm late afternoon and the park was filled with people. The first thing the girls noticed were crowds gathered in circles. One crowd watched a juggler tossing burning torches in the air while sitting on a unicycle. Stevie put a quarter in his hat.

"Isn't that the quarter you're supposed to use to call Max if we can't find our way home?" Lisa asked.

"Sure, it is," Stevie said. "But who cares if we ever find our way home? I *love* this place! And look, something else is going on over there!"

They went over to the next crowd and found a group of four men dressed as the Beatles doing old Beatles songs.

"I wish Dad could see this!" Carole said. "They're great!" Carole's father loved old music from the fifties and sixties.

"There's another crowd!" Lisa said, tugging at her friends' sleeves. "Let's see what's going on over there."

The threesome walked to the other side of the big fountain in the center of the park to see why a crowd had gathered. It was a bigger crowd than any of the others. As they got closer, they could see that the ground was almost covered with thick black electrical wires. There was a small section of railroad track and on it was a little seat and camera.

Someone was making a movie!

On further examination, they realized that the whole area of the park was roped off. Six trailers were lined up at the edge of the park, and nearby, in the park, there were empty director's chairs with names printed across the backs.

"Hey, if we can read the names, we can see who's in the movie," Stevie said, edging around.

"We could ask, too," Carole suggested.

"Yeah, we *could*," Stevie said, but she continued to move toward the chairs.

Lisa didn't have to. She knew what movie was being filmed in New York and she knew who was starring in it.

"It's Skye Ransom's movie, *City Cowboy*," she informed her friends.

"Do you think?" Stevie asked. She squinted at the chairs. An astonished look crossed her face. "How did you know?" she asked.

"It just had to be," Lisa explained. "Remember when we were talking about Skye and how his movie is being filmed in New York? If we wait long enough, we'll probably see Skye Ransom in person."

"There's no guarantee of that," Carole reminded Lisa. "And there goes a pizza being delivered to one of the trailers over there. That must be where they have the wardrobe and makeup rooms—and the stars' dressing rooms, too! If they're getting pizza, they must be on dinner break. No way we can wait until their break is over. Max will have kittens if we're late. I think Dorothy's taking us to Chinatown for dinner."

"No problem." Lisa shrugged. "This trip is perfect, so I just know our paths will cross. It's fate!"

Stevie glanced over at Carole and they both laughed. Lisa wasn't usually this excitable.

"Anyway," Lisa continued, "we can come back tomorrow morning and we'll see Skye Ransom then, for sure. For now, we'd better go back to Dorothy's." She consulted the map again. "This way!" she said, and led her friends through the rest of the maze of the park—

past another juggler, a rhythm-and-blues band, and the most unlikely collection of chess players they'd ever seen.

Her new haircut bounced as she walked. She liked the feel of it. In fact, she liked everything about New York.

4

THE NEXT DAY began with a big disappointment for
The Saddle Club. They were up and out of the house
before breakfast. Lisa just had to get back to Washington Square Park for a glimpse of Skye Ransom on
the set. Carole and Stevie came along, as eager as Lisa
to see their idol.

The park was almost totally empty at that early
hour. Not only were there no jugglers and musicians,
but there were no wires, lights, director's chairs, or
trailers. It was clear at a glance that they were not
going to see Skye Ransom at work in the park.

"Oh, drat," Stevie said. "Maybe we should have
stayed yesterday."

"If we'd stayed yesterday, Max would *still* be yelling
at us," Carole reminded her. "We didn't really have a
choice."

"She's right," Lisa told Stevie, but she wished it were not true.

Dejected, the three girls returned to Dorothy's. They found the adults discussing the day's plan.

"The show doesn't really start until tomorrow," Dorothy was saying. "And when I told the Mallendorfs you were coming up for a visit, they insisted on taking us out on their boat. The trouble is, they just don't have room for the girls to come, too."

"Well, we'll just have to cancel, then," Max said. "We certainly can't leave the girls here alone."

"Max, whatever turned you into such an overbearing fuddy-duddy?" Dorothy asked. Stevie hid a smile. Max seemed to be taking the weight of the responsibility for The Saddle Club very seriously. He was turning into a worrywart before their very eyes.

"Well, if anything happened to them . . ." he began.

"Nothing's going to happen," Dorothy assured him. "You wouldn't be worried if they were spending the day on horses, would you?"

"Of course not," Max said. "They know what they're doing on horses!"

"That's just what I thought you'd say and so it's what I arranged." She turned to the girls. "You brought riding clothes, didn't you?" The girls nodded. "All right. I've made arrangements for you to ride in Central Park today. The owner of the stables is my friend and I've guaranteed him you girls know what you're doing on horses." She turned back to Max. "Satisfied?" she asked.

He smiled at her. "You always could outfox me, you know. And I have a certain grudging admiration for any student of mine who thinks she knows more than I do. I give up. You're in charge of this ragtag bunch of riders. You're going to win all the arguments anyway, so go ahead. Make plans without consulting me."

"Don't worry. I will," Dorothy said. Then she winked at the girls.

The girls changed into their riding clothes. Dorothy gave them complete instructions on how to get to the stable and what to expect, then gave them money for taxis (and lessons on tipping). Dorothy's mother wasn't going on the boat trip, so she'd be home to let the girls in when they got back.

Max put them in a taxi. Stevie was relieved to see that he refrained from giving them another long list of "don'ts." Apparently, when he'd relented to Dorothy, he'd meant it. All he said was that they should have fun—and they already intended to do that.

They soon discovered that a stable in New York was very different from one in Willow Creek. This one was actually an old garage. It had no pasture and no paddocks. They looked around while the owner talked to another new rider. The ring was indoors. It was dark and small. The horses were apparently housed both above and below the ring. The girls expected to tack up their horses, but they saw that when other people's horses arrived, the tack was already on. Everything had been done but tightening the girths. The riders were not even allowed in the stabling area.

"What a way to go!" Stevie said.

"I don't know," Carole said. "I sort of think taking care of the horse, like tacking up, is part of riding. It's nice to have somebody else do the work sometimes, but I think I'd miss it if I never got to tack up."

"Feel the same way about mucking out?" Stevie asked.

"Well . . . I think I can draw the line there," Carole said quickly, laughing. Nobody liked mucking out—not even horse crazy people.

The owner glanced up at them questioningly, and they introduced themselves. He was expecting them. He looked them over carefully, as if he could tell whether they were good riders by the way they stood in the waiting area. Dorothy had promised him that the girls were skilled riders and definitely trustworthy. The look on his face showed doubt.

"But Dorothy said you girls were good and if anybody knows what she's talking about, Dorothy DeSoto does. Besides, I'm too busy now to spend time second-guessing Dorothy. Your horses will be down in a few minutes. Your instructor is Marta. She's the one in the green pants, over there in the ring."

They left the office and walked through the soft dirt that covered the ring's concrete floor and introduced themselves to their instructor. It was not that they really needed or wanted a lesson, but this was not Willow Creek and they were not permitted into Central Park without an instructor—at least not until they'd proved to Marta that they were good riders.

Marta was really nice. She told the girls that she'd been riding since she was a little girl and all she'd ever wanted to do was to ride. She came from Ohio, where she could ride all the time, and when her husband had gotten a job in New York, she didn't know what she'd do. She'd been pleased to learn that people actually ride horses in the city.

"There's your horse, Carole," she said, pointing to a pinto who lumbered up the stairs from the basement.

Stevie's and Lisa's horses arrived from upstairs a few minutes later. Stevie was on a bay and Lisa's was a roan. Marta was riding a big chestnut. When everybody had mounted, the owner opened the big electric garage door and they were off.

The park was a few blocks from the stable. They walked slowly, obeying the traffic laws. Stevie was unsettled by the cars whizzing by, to say nothing of the sirens and the noises of garbage trucks. The horses didn't seem to notice. Stevie asked Marta about it.

"Oh, these horses have seen it all," she said. "They know about New York traffic—even the crazy drivers. They *might* act up if they hear something weird like a crow cawing, but an itty-bitty siren won't worry them at all."

Stevie knew Marta was joking, but she also knew that Marta was right. Her horse was as calm as could be. It gave her some confidence.

Central Park was in the heart of Manhattan. Stevie knew it as a big square of green on a map, and now she was greeting it in person for the first time. It wasn't quite what she'd expected.

"We'll go around the top end of the reservoir first," Marta said. "We can walk and trot most places, but we have to be careful where we canter. Some of the bridle path is sort of rocky and that's rough on the horses' hooves. Therefore, no cantering without my okay. Deal?"

"Of course," Carole assured her. "We wouldn't want to hurt the horses."

"I wish all the riders felt that way," Marta said. "A lot of them think all there is to riding is kicking the belly and yanking at the reins. The horses get pretty tired of that, I can tell you. Now, let's ride."

With that, they began the ride. Stevie shifted her weight to signal her horse to begin and they were off.

LISA WAS SO content riding in the park that she forgot her disappointment at not seeing Skye Ransom in Washington Square Park that morning. It seemed to her that the trip was perfect enough, in spite of that letdown.

She liked the horse she was riding. She had been riding long enough to know that every horse was different from others, in physical ability as well as personality. This one—his name was Mickey—had seemed a little tense when she'd first gotten on him. Now, she could feel that he was more relaxed and responsive. Considering the variety of riders he'd probably had, she wasn't really surprised. She'd learned that horses tended to test riders they did not know. Once the rider had shown the horse who was boss, the horse could relax and follow orders. Mickey now did what she told him to with her legs and her hands. She could just relax and enjoy the ride.

Central Park was really very pretty. The bridle path wound through wooded and grassy areas, passing by playing fields and ponds. There were lots of people in the park, too. Joggers trotted around the lake, and dog-walkers were everywhere. There were a few other riders on the path as well.

Lisa observed them critically. One woman passed them coming the other way. She was in total control of her horse. Obviously, she was an expert. At the other end of the spectrum, there were two riders behind them on the path who seemed almost out of control. One was a man. The other was a boy, probably a couple of years older than she was, Lisa thought. She'd only gotten a glimpse of him, but the boy was sitting on the horse all wrong. Lisa hoped he got some control, or he was going to be in trouble.

"We can canter for about a hundred yards up ahead," Marta said. Mickey's ears perked up. It was as

if he understood the word. Lisa could feel his muscles
flex in preparation. They began trotting and then, as
soon as the path was smooth, Mickey broke into a canter.

Stevie and Carole began cantering, as did Marta,
but Lisa wasn't happy with the fact that Mickey had
made his own decision about gait. She knew it was not
a good idea to let the horse do the thinking. He had to
remember who was the boss. She reined him in. A
little reluctantly, it seemed, Mickey stopped. He
watched longingly as his friends cantered on ahead
with Lisa's friends.

"I'm in charge here," Lisa said to him. She knew
he could not understand the words, but he would understand her tone of voice. "Now, we're going to walk
first, then trot, then canter, when *I* say so, understand?"

Mickey stood obediently until she shifted her
weight in the saddle, signaling him to start walking.
Carole, Stevie, and Marta were well ahead of her, but
they would understand. And, after all, Lisa told herself, the path was really just a circle, wasn't it? She'd
catch up with them. For now, taking the time to repri-
mand Mickey was more important than cantering
freely.

She put a little pressure on Mickey's sides with her
legs and he promptly began to trot. "Good boy," she
said, rewarding his behavior. She sat the trot, rather
than posting, since she was about to canter.

It was then that Lisa heard the fast hoofbeats of a canter behind her. Mickey heard it, too. His ears lay flat back on his head and he tensed immediately. Lisa shortened up on the reins. Horses were naturally competitive and did not like to have other horses pass them. It would not take much to get Mickey to canter, too, but Lisa did not want to have him make any independent decisions right then. She had to stay in charge.

The other horse was very close now, and then Lisa could hear that his rider was shouting something. The words were indistinct, but the message was clear: "Help!"

Without looking, Lisa knew what had happened. The young rider behind her had totally lost control and his horse was running away with him. He was right: He *needed* help.

The other horse and rider flew by. Lisa touched Mickey behind the girth and he spurted into a canter. The other rider was ahead, but Mickey had a lot of pent-up energy and Lisa was pretty sure they'd catch up.

"Hold on!" she yelled to the other rider. "Keep your balance and try to grip with your legs!"

She knew her instructions were right, but they weren't doing much good. The boy was bouncing all over the horse's back. "Shorten up on the reins!" she yelled, but then she saw he could not do that. He'd dropped the reins altogether. "Grab the mane!"

He did that.

The boy's horse veered off the main path onto a footpath that meandered through several baseball diamonds. Lisa followed. She was vaguely aware that the boy's companion was behind her, and she hoped he'd help, too.

Then, the boy's horse came to an uphill section. Instinctively, the horse approached it sideways for his own safety. It was the one chance Lisa would have to beat the frantic runaway. She gave Mickey the command and he followed it, going straight up the hill at full tilt. It worked. She and Mickey beat the runaway to the summit!

The runaway took one look at Mickey and Lisa and came to a sudden halt, unceremoniously dumping his rider onto the grassy knoll. The boy's hat came loose and fell down over his face. He grunted.

Before dismounting, Lisa reached over and grabbed the runaway's reins. She did not want him to take off again. Then, as quickly as possible, she dismounted. Still holding the reins, she knelt down by the boy's side. He was breathing okay and that was a relief. She removed the hat to be sure he was all right, and found herself looking straight into the very familiar face of Skye Ransom.

5

"OH, MY!" LISA said, and then wished immediately that she hadn't. She thought it made her sound very dumb, which she wasn't, instead of dumbstruck, which she was. She removed her riding hat, collected her thoughts, and spoke. "You're Skye Ransom, aren't you?"

"Guilty as charged," he said, sitting up slowly. He winced and rubbed his shoulder. "Hey, I like the haircut," he said, his admiring glance taking in Lisa's new hairdo. "But who are you?"

For a second, she was so flustered by his compliment that she almost couldn't remember her own name. She ran her fingers through her hair, stalling. "I'm . . . ah, uh." That sounded even dumber to her than her earlier "Oh, my!" She swallowed and then the words came out in a flood. "I'm Lisa Atwood. And I thought you could ride. I read this article about the movie you're making and I know it said you would be riding a horse, but it didn't look to me as if you knew what you were doing, do you?"

"Obviously not, huh?" he said, and then tried to stand. She offered him a hand. He accepted it, pulled himself up, and began dusting off the dirt that had smeared onto his pants and jacket. "Riding looks so easy when other people do it," he continued. "I thought it would be a breeze, so I told the studio I could ride. But it isn't true. I can't ride at all. I was watching you and your friends ride in front of us. You girls made it look easy. You even made it look fun."

"But it *is*. Both of them, I mean. It's also a lot of work." Lisa studied the hand that he had held. It looked the same, but it felt different. It was her right hand. Skye Ransom had actually held her right hand! She felt a nice shiver and then she came to her senses.

Lisa handed Skye his horse's reins. He looked at them as if he'd never seen them before, and never wanted to see them again. Then he looked pleadingly at Lisa. She realized that Skye Ransom was asking her for help. She smiled at him to reassure him and then began helping.

"You just got off on the wrong foot," Lisa said. "You started riding without knowing what you were doing. Now you're going to start again, only this time you'll know what you're doing because I'm going to teach you."

"I don't think I should ride any more," Skye said, offering her the reins back.

"And *I* think you should ride a *lot* more," Lisa said. "You've heard the one about getting back on the horse, haven't you? Well, it's absolutely true. Now here's how you mount." She told Skye how to hold the reins, mane, and saddle when he mounted his horse. He was reluctant at first, but listened to Lisa's advice. With her step-by-step instructions, Skye was in the saddle by the time his riding companion joined them. Skye introduced him to Lisa as his manager, Frank Nelson.

"I thought you fell!" Mr. Nelson said.

"I did," Skye told him. "But Lisa here got me back on."

Mr. Nelson looked at her dubiously. "She knows what she's doing," Skye said. "She's really good."

"But will she *tell*?" Mr. Nelson asked.

"No way!" Skye said. "Will you, Lisa?"

"You mean, do I want to see your face and mine on a newspaper at the supermarket check-out counter with a headline like, Little Lisa Reveals Big Skye's Secret: He Can't Ride!" Mr. Nelson's face paled visibly, and Lisa realized that was exactly what he had meant, and to him it was no joke. "No," she assured both of them. "Your secret is safe with me." She heard more hoofbeats coming up behind them. "And my friends," she concluded.

"Lisa! Are you okay?" Carole asked.

Lisa wanted to tell them that she'd probably never been better in her whole life, but she decided that would be silly—and unnecessary. Both girls and Marta recognized Skye at the same instant and their jaws dropped.

There was a silence and Lisa decided to fill it with the rest of Skye's first riding lesson. She helped him adjust the reins so he was holding them properly and then she showed him how to signal the horse to begin walking.

"Sit up straight," she said. "Legs should be relaxed but close. Heels down, wrists should be flexible, hold your hands lower. Now, look where you want the horse to go. It helps with steering and balance. Don't jiggle your legs. The horse thinks you mean something."

Skye listened carefully and Lisa could tell that he was trying to follow every piece of instruction she was giving him. Mr. Nelson was trying to do the same.

Soon, with Lisa's good instructions, they were moving easily with their horses at a walk, and the six riders returned to the bridle path together.

"Good work," Lisa said.

"This isn't work, this is easy," Skye told her.

"Well, when you're doing it right, it *is* easy. It's just that sometimes it's hard to do it right."

"You know, from some people, what you just said wouldn't make any sense at all, but when you say it, I know exactly what you mean. You're a natural teacher."

Lisa pinched herself. Not only was she actually talking to *the* Skye Ransom, but he liked her hair and he liked the way she taught. She decided that she had been right that this trip to New York was perfect and nothing would go wrong. There was a magic spell over the whole adventure. It would not last, of course, but for now, there *was* magic. It was the only explanation.

Mr. Nelson said he had an appointment and had to get back to the stable. "Ah, come on, Frank," Skye protested. "I'm just getting the hang of it."

Marta glanced at Mr. Nelson. "I have to head back too, for a lesson. But I'm sure these girls could safely deliver Skye back to the stables."

"No problem," Stevie assured her. "This is a job The Saddle Club can handle, with pleasure."

"What's The Saddle Club?" Skye asked as Marta and Mr. Nelson headed back to the stable. They told him.

"So far, I'm not eligible for membership," he said. "It turns out that I'm not horse crazy, I'm just *plain* crazy. I'm scared to death of this animal, but I've got to learn to be a good rider, by the end of the week!"

"No way," Carole said. "Riding is something you learn over months and years, not days."

"There's going to have to be an exception in my case," Skye said. "See, we're filming the horse sequences in just a few days. I don't actually have to be a championship rider, I just have to *look* like one and I think it's going to be the challenge of my acting career!"

"You're doing okay walking," Carole told him.

"Great, but in the movie, I have to go really fast—

like this horse was doing before, only I have to stay on it! Do you suppose the cameramen could film me walking and then speed it up so it looks like he's running?"

"The gait is called cantering," Lisa told him. "And unfortunately, a canter isn't a fast walk, any more than a person jogging is fast walking. It looks entirely different. I suppose you could take a slow canter and make it look like a fast canter, but that's about it."

"Okay, so how do I learn years' worth in a week?"

"You need a really good teacher," Lisa said.

"And total secrecy," he added. "See, part of my contract is my guarantee that I can ride. On second thought, what I really need is a miracle. Does The Saddle Club do miracles?"

"You know," Lisa said, looking at her friends. "Max is the best teacher in the world, maybe—"

"Oh, Max would never have the time!" Stevie said quickly.

"But he loves instructing," Lisa said, giving her a look. "And if we asked him, you know, specially—"

"No way." Carole cut her off. "And besides, Max is the wrong teacher for Skye. His temperament is all wrong for this kind of pressure."

Lisa thought she saw Carole wink at Stevie and she wondered why.

"What's wrong with Max's temperament? He's strict, sure, but—"

"And Max would never agree to take on an inexperienced student like Skye," Stevie said firmly.

53

"But he has a lot of inex—"

"Max is going to be way too busy coaching Dorothy this week," Carole said. "Remember?"

At first, Lisa could not figure out what her friends were talking about. Max was a great teacher. He liked working with beginners, and he wasn't coaching Dorothy at all. Were her friends trying to ruin Skye's chances? Then it hit her.

"They're right," she said to Skye. "Max is good all right, but it won't work this week. He's just too busy. We, on the other hand, have lots of time. In fact, The Saddle Club just took a vote, and every minute that we're not actually at the American Horse Show and that you're not on a set can be devoted to instructing you in the fine art of looking like a really good rider."

"You mean you'd teach me on your own?"

"Sure," Stevie said. "It won't get you a blue ribbon at a horse show, but by the end of a couple of lessons, you won't be an embarrassment."

"And we won't tell, either," Lisa added with a smile.

"Anyone?" he asked.

That was going to be tough. If they were actually going to spend a lot of time with Skye Ransom, how could they not tell the whole world? They looked at one another. Stevie shrugged and spoke for all of them.

"We're not really giving up anything, you guys," she said. "Who would believe us, anyway?" she asked.

Carole, Lisa, and Skye laughed. The deal was made.

They agreed to meet at the stable the following morning at eight-thirty.

The Saddle Club couldn't wait!

6

"I DON'T THINK I slept one minute last night," Lisa confessed to her friends on their way to the stable the next morning.

"Me, neither," Stevie said. "All I could think about was Skye Ransom. Those eyes, his cute nose—I mean, even his ears . . ." Stevie sighed.

"But mostly how *nice* he is," Lisa continued. "He's so friendly, and so, I don't know, just normal. Can you believe this whole thing?"

"I believe it," Carole said. "All *I* could think about is how much he has to learn about riding in how little time! This is no joke, you know."

Lisa knew that Carole was right, but nothing could ruin her own giddy mood.

"I think our goal should be to build Skye's confidence in himself," Carole began.

"You sound like the way my mother talked after she

read some dumb self-help book," Stevie said. "And besides, Skye Ransom is about the most famous movie star there is. How can he need self-confidence?"

"It's not self-confidence he needs," Carole explained. "It's confidence in his ability to manage a horse and ride. You know—you-can-if-you-think-you-can."

"Now *that* sounds like the way I took piano lessons," Lisa said. "I hardly ever practiced, so I just assumed I could do the work at my lessons."

"And?" Stevie asked expectantly.

"It didn't work," Lisa explained. "So I gave up the piano altogether and began working very hard at learning to ride. I'm much better at riding than I ever was at piano and I know it's because I do work hard and I do practice."

The girls got to the stable before Skye. They arranged for their horses and his so that by the time he arrived, they were in the ring, ready to mount.

Skye stepped out of the office and walked toward them. He was wearing breeches and high boots. He carried a black velvet-covered riding hat in one hand and a riding crop in the other. He tapped the riding crop up against his leg impatiently as he walked. Lisa almost held her breath watching him. The effect of the dress riding clothes, hat, and crop made Skye look as if he'd been riding all of his life. Lisa could hardly believe he was the same boy who had fallen so badly the day before. He looked like he had more confidence

than the entire U.S. Equestrian Team put together—
until he got near his horse.

"Is that one mine?" he asked. "He looks so *big*."

"*He* is a *she*," Carole explained politely. "She's a
mare named Cinnamon and she's about fifteen
hands—which isn't considered big for a horse."

"Hand? What does that mean?"

"It's the traditional way of measuring horses," Stevie explained. "A 'hand' is four inches—approx-
imately the width of a person's hand across the palm.
The horse is measured at the withers, which is what
the part right at the end of the mane is called. You
could think of withers as being shoulders. Anyway, if
you translate hands to feet, you'll see that Cinnamon is
sixty inches, and that's just five feet."

"So we can rule out a basketball career for her?" he
joked.

Lisa laughed a little even though she didn't think
the joke was very funny. In spite of the swagger in his
walk, she thought Skye was nervous. She hoped that
laughing at his joke would make him feel better. It
didn't.

Skye held Cinnamon's reins nervously. He eyed the
saddle, and Lisa thought she knew exactly what was
going through his head. He didn't want to climb up.
He didn't want to ride. Mostly, he didn't want to end
up in the grass again. He looked Cinnamon in the eye.
Cinnamon stared back at him, blankly. He took a ten-
tative step forward. Cinnamon responded by stepping

back one step. They stared at each other again. If it was to be a game of chicken, Lisa had the awful feeling Cinnamon would win.

"Remember how I showed you to hold the reins and mount yesterday, Skye?" Lisa asked, breaking up the staring contest between horse and rider. He shook his head.

Lisa walked over to her horse to demonstrate, easily swinging her right leg up and over the saddle. Skye tried to follow her example, but ended up sliding right off the other side. He dusted himself off, circled around to Cinnamon's left side again, and studied his target. The look of fear on his face was gone. It had been replaced by determination. He took the reins, grasped the saddle, and hoisted himself up. It wasn't smooth or beautiful, but he was on top of the horse, and that was progress.

"You'll get better at that," Lisa assured him. "Practice does it. For now, the important thing is that you're in the saddle and we're ready to go."

Skye smiled at her and she had the feeling that he was summoning all of his acting skills to smile at that moment.

One of the stable hands opened the doors to the street, and the four riders turned their horses to leave the stable and head for New York's Central Park. Lisa nudged her horse, a big bay gelding, and he responded eagerly. He wanted to get out into the park and have a nice ride.

Cinnamon, on the other hand, had apparently decided that the stable was a nicer place to be, especially if she didn't have to pay any attention to her rider. While Lisa watched, Skye nudged his horse's belly. She merely sighed. He waggled the reins. She shook her head. He kicked her belly. She took a step forward and then stopped. "Giddyup!" he said. She looked at him over her shoulder.

"Use the riding crop on her," Lisa suggested. "Don't hit her hard, just use it to remind her who is in charge."

Skye tapped Cinnamon on her flank. It worked to a certain degree. She began walking slowly, but when he tried to get her to turn right to exit, she headed left.

"Maybe this isn't such a good idea after all," Skye said to Lisa. "I mean, maybe Cinnamon really deserves a morning in her nice comfortable stable instead of running all over the park, dumping me in fields, you know?"

Lisa looked at him and knew at that moment that he was absolutely serious. And she couldn't help it. She burst into laughter.

"It's not funny," he said, a little hurt.

"I'm sorry," Lisa said, still giggling. "But it won't be funny if you get fired from the movie because the director learns you're a phony, will it?"

Skye shook his head, and Lisa knew she had found

the key. "Okay, let's go," he agreed. "I'm ready to learn."

"Good," Lisa said. "Because we're ready to teach. Now, first of all, let's get out of here."

Once again, she showed Skye how to hold the reins and how to signal the horse to move so that the horse knew he meant business.

"You have to make Cinnamon do what you want her to," Lisa explained. "Most horses are willing to obey their riders, but before they start doing everything you say, they want to know you *mean* it. That's why it's really important to make her follow your instructions. If you let her take one step forward when you've already told her to stay still, she'll try taking two the next time and then three, then you'll never be able to control her. I guess I mean it's important to win the little battles so you never get into the big ones."

Skye listened intently. He took a firm hold of the reins and aimed Cinnamon at the door. It worked. Their horses walked down the ramp and onto the city street. The four riders headed for the park. Cinnamon seemed to relax now that it was clear they had a goal. She knew the way to the park better than Skye did. The girls chatted with Skye as the horses walked easily, winding through the double-parked cars.

"Our plan for today is to take you up through a trot," Carole said. "You'll need to know how to balance yourself and how to post and then—"

"But all I have to learn is how to canter," Skye said. "I don't really have to trot, too, do I?"

"Oh, sure!" Carole responded instantly. "Trotting's really important. And it's essential to be able to trot before you learn cantering. That's our goal, right, to have you be able to canter before the shoot at the end of the week?"

Skye nodded, but he didn't speak right then because he was busy reining Cinnamon in. They'd come to a red light and the girls had stopped their horses. Cinnamon, however, seemed to want to keep going. Skye hauled back on the reins, pulling them into his chest.

It was hard to believe, but Skye Ransom—cool, suave Skye Ransom, the cute guy with the beautiful eyes, sweet nose, and even lovable ears—looked totally awkward yanking at Cinnamon's reins. Lisa knew there was a *lot* of work to do.

"How much time are we going to have today?" she asked. "I mean, when do you have to be on the set?" She liked saying "on the set." It sounded so exciting.

"I'm not due on the set until late this afternoon," he said. "I was planning on riding until about four—"

"Oh, no way!" Stevie said. "You can't do that much riding, and we have to be at the show by noon."

"Well, if you have to go, it's okay," Skye said. "I'll just keep on after you go."

"That's not what I meant," Stevie said. "First of all, you are going to be *so* sore!" All the girls laughed.

"And you can only learn so much in one day, probably about two hours' worth. So, we should ride some today, some tomorrow, some the next day. It's like a little bit goes a long way."

The light changed and the four of them proceeded into the park. The horses seemed to become more lively as soon as they reached the bridle path. Lisa loved it when she could feel her horse get excited about riding. The bay tensed, eager to get going. Cinnamon did the same thing, too. Lisa could tell by the whiteness of Skye's knuckles grasping the horse's reins.

"Relax," she said. "This is the fun part."

She didn't hear his answer.

Carole took over as teacher in charge of Skye. Stevie led the group, Carole and Skye came next. Lisa brought up the rear. Since Carole was the best rider and had the most experience working with new riders, including both Stevie and Lisa when they had just started, she was the best teacher. Lisa watched, remembering.

Riding had become so natural to Lisa that she'd almost forgotten what it was like to be as scared as Skye, and as ignorant. She watched while Carole demonstrated posting, showing Skye what to do with his hands, and what not to do with them. She was carefully preparing him to trot his horse. She was also preparing him to canter, but he didn't even know it. One thing Lisa had learned was that riding knowledge was cumulative. Everything you learned was necessary to know before you could learn the next thing.

Stevie, at the front, had set the pace at a walk. When the path opened up, she began trotting.

"Are you ready?" Carole asked Skye. He shrugged.

"Either you are ready or you're not," Carole said sternly. "If you want to do something, we'll do it. If you don't, we'll wait. *You* are the one in charge, both of the pace of this lesson, and of your horse."

He looked sheepish. "Well, I have the feeling I ought to trot, but I'm not really sure I understand about posting. Can you show me again before we trot?"

Carole smiled and glanced over her shoulder at Lisa. "He's learning!" she announced proudly. It was true, too. Lisa knew that a real sign of learning was not being afraid to ask for help. Carole then carefully went through the description of posting. As she demonstrated posting, she brought her horse to a trot. In a perfectly natural way, to keep up with Carole, Skye got his horse to trot, too, and probably before he knew what he was doing, he began trotting—and posting.

"Up, down. Up, down," Carole chanted.

Lisa watched, proud as a parent. Carole was a wonderful teacher and she was right: Skye was learning a lot.

"Heels down, calves in," Carole instructed him. "Now bring your hands in toward your hips. Hold them steady. Eyes forward, loosen up those knees."

Every time Carole gave an instruction, Skye tried to follow it. Lisa could see that he'd follow it all right, but he'd immediately forget all the other instructions she'd given. As soon as his calves gripped the horse, his heels bounced up. Hands came in okay, but his legs would start flopping. Lisa smiled to herself. It was hard to follow a dozen instructions at once!

Carole was tireless, though. "Shoulders back, chin up. No, no, hold your hands in place. You're not on a merry-go-round horse! If you waggle the reins like that the horse gets confused. Heels down! Watch the angle of your knees! Forearms parallel to the ground! Square the shoulders!"

"What is this? A geometry lesson?" Skye asked, struggling with the instructions. Carole laughed at his joke, but she didn't let it interrupt the lesson. She brought him and Cinnamon to a halt and went over proper riding position again. Lisa could see that he was trying very hard, but she knew that these weren't things a rider could learn in a day, no matter how hard he worked.

When Carole thought he was ready to move again, they began trotting. It wasn't show form. It wasn't even very good form, but it was better form, and that was good enough for his first lesson. Carole sighed with relief.

It was Stevie's turn. She worked with him on stops and starts and subtle signals.

"Horses really like it better if you don't kick them or yank at the reins," Stevie said. Then she spent some time working with Skye on hand, leg, and crop signals. At first, he got terribly confused and couldn't remember whether he was supposed to press or release to tell Cinnamon to speed up.

"Look, some of this will only come with time," Stevie said. "We don't have a lot of it so pretend you've been taking lessons for six months instead of a few hours, okay?"

Skye smiled at her joke. Lisa thought it was probably his first real smile of the day.

"Okay, so when I want him, I mean her, to move, I sit down into the saddle. Then, when I want her to stop, I sit down into the saddle. And, if I want to turn, I sit down into the saddle? Seems pretty clear-cut to me—as long as Cinnamon is a mind reader!" Skye said. He sounded like he was joking, but the exasperation was clear.

"Did I say that?" Stevie asked Lisa.

"More or less," Lisa said. Then she turned to Skye. "The worst part is that it's about true. I think it would be helpful to remember that the horse's back is sensitive, and when you shift the way you sit in the saddle, it alerts the horse that something's up. Then when you add another small signal . . ."

Lisa saw the confused look on Skye's face and tried to explain it in another way he might understand. "Listen, you're an actor—you know how important your small gestures are to an audience. Sometimes, something like a raised eyebrow can mean a whole lot more than if you're jumping all over the stage." She paused, and Skye grinned.

"*And* if you combine a raised eyebrow with another small gesture like shrugging your shoulders, it can mean something very different," Lisa continued. "Well, it's the same with horses. Small signals are very important in riding. If you combine a weight shift with a leg or hand signal, it tells the horse you mean business. Does that make more sense?"

Skye thought for a while. "I suppose so," he said. His tone was one of resigned determination. Lisa sensed it was time to quit for the day. There was no way he could soak in as much information as he'd already gotten, so giving him more wasn't going to do any good.

"Let's give him a break now, guys, okay?" Lisa suggested. That made Skye smile again. "It's time to go back to the stable."

The group walked their horses together and chatted. As long as the subject was horses, The Saddle Club never ran out of things to talk about. Carole reminded the girls that they'd better hurry after their ride to be sure to get to the horse show by the time the afternoon session began.

"You're really going to it?" Skye asked.

The girls nodded. "Oh, yes!" Carole said. "That's why we're really here—to watch Dorothy DeSoto jump. She's really famous, and a former student of our teacher, Max. And you know, you should come, too! It would be a great way for you to learn—especially an actor like you. You're really good at imitating things you've seen. Like the way you swaggered when you came into the stable today, slapping your leg with your crop. Imagine what you can learn from *real* riders."

"She's right," Stevie told him. "It would be great experience for you—and it would be too dangerous trying to ride by yourself this afternoon. Besides, you'll be very sore where you sit down if you try to ride any more today, anyway."

Skye looked at Lisa to see if the vote was unanimous. "I agree," Lisa said, smiling at him. "This is going to be my first real horse show, but I've learned a lot watching good riders—and these are the best."

"Well, you've convinced me," Skye said. "We'll go to the horse show together. And if it turns out that the best part about it is that sitting *there* means I'm not sitting *here*,"—he pointed to the saddle—"that's still good enough for me!"

The four of them laughed as they walked their horses out of the park to return to the stable. Lisa thought, as they walked back, how lucky she was. Not only was she horse crazy, but she had lots of opportunities to ride. Poor Skye. Not only was he not horse crazy, but he *had* to ride even when he didn't want to. She remembered how she'd hated having to take piano and ballet lessons. But when you loved something— like riding—you didn't care how much you had to practice. Lisa hoped that seeing the championship riders at the show would help give him the inspiration he'd need, because without inspiration, he wasn't ever going to fool anybody about his riding.

7

THE GIRLS DECIDED to wear their street clothes to the horse show. Skye would wear his riding clothes. He looked a little funny traveling around the city in breeches, high boots, and a velvet-covered hat, but as Stevie pointed out, it accomplished two things. In the first place, nobody recognized him. Secondly, everybody at Madison Square Garden would assume he was a competitor and let him straight in. The girls had their passes. They had already agreed to meet Max and Mrs. Reg in the stable area by noon.

Getting there by noon was no trouble. Skye's studio had provided him with an enormous black limousine, which was waiting outside the stables when they returned from the park.

"Wow!" the girls said in one breath as the driver hopped out to open the door for Skye.

"Well," Lisa said reluctantly, "I guess we'll meet you at the horse show—"

"Are you kidding?" Skye interrupted. "You've got to come with me!"

Stevie didn't need to be asked twice. "All right!" she crowed as she bounded inside the stretch limousine. Carole followed more sedately, but her dark eyes were wide and shining. When Lisa slid in behind her, Stevie whispered, "I wish Miss Veronica diAngelo could see us now. She'd be absolutely green!" Laughing, The Saddle Club agreed that it was true. Veronica was a snobby girl who rode at Pine Hollow Stables. Just because her father owned the local bank, she acted as if he owned the whole town, too!

Skye joined them, and the car pulled smoothly away from the curb. "All set?" he asked the girls.

"You bet!" Stevie answered for them.

Lisa just smiled and leaned back against the soft leather seats. So this is what it felt like to be famous. She could get used to this. Definitely.

AFTER THE SADDLE Club girls got tired of staring out the windows at the city streets, the foursome settled back and watched game shows on the car's television. Stevie rooted around in the mini refrigerator for some sodas and Skye found some munchies. All too soon the driver pulled up in front of the side entrance of Madison Square Garden.

"Life in Willow Creek is going to be so *dull* after

this!" Stevie complained, stepping out of the limo. She saw that there was a small group of people who had paused on the sidewalk, hoping for a glance at someone famous who might emerge from the limousine. Several people looked at her curiously. It was all the encouragement she needed. She smiled brightly. They smiled back. She nodded and then waved. They waved back. Behind her, Lisa, Carole, and Skye exited from the limo and headed for the side door.

"Thanks for the lift," Skye said to Stevie loud enough for people to hear it. That made them think it really *was* Stevie's car. It was her cue and she wrote the script as she went along.

"Anytime," Stevie said graciously. "As a matter of fact, you can have this old car. See, the Porsche's been in the shop but the new Rolls arrives tomorrow . . ."

The crowd around Stevie got bigger. They looked at her in awe. She added cars to her repertoire. ". . . and the Corvette? Well, the brakes were really shot. I mean, when you need a Lamborghini, a Corvette just won't do!" Somehow, Stevie kept a straight face. She was about to launch into a monologue on the advantages of her small jet over her large one when a girl about her own age stepped out of the crowd.

"Can I have your autograph?" the girl asked, offering Stevie a piece of paper and a stub of pencil.

"Oh, sure," Stevie said. She took the paper, signed it, and handed it back to the girl. She then followed her friends through the doorway to the horse show. As soon as the door closed behind her, the girls and Skye exploded in laughter.

"You were *wonderful!*" Skye said in frank admiration. That made Stevie feel good because she was sure it was true.

"What's that girl going to think when she sees she's got Stevie Lake's autograph?" Lisa asked.

"Oh, but she doesn't have Stevie Lake's autograph at all," Stevie told her friends. "See, I signed it 'Princess Di'!"

They were laughing so hard that they didn't pay much attention to where they were going through the back halls of Madison Square Garden. They walked right into the Rangers' dressing room. Even though there were no Rangers in sight, an usher chased them out and shooed them in the right direction.

ALTHOUGH THEY WERE walking into the same stable area they'd visited only two days before, Carole would have sworn it was a whole new place—not because it looked any different. It didn't. It just *felt* different. It was because the competition had begun. Riders, trainers, and grooms moved about quickly and efficiently. It was the time for last-minute crises and nerves. Carole could almost smell the tension.

Riders and grooms were doing serious grooming on their horses. They wanted their horses to gleam, like never before. The tack around the stable area was spotless. Lint and dirt was being swept off the riders' jackets and pants. A smudge on a boot, usually just a routine part of riding, was viewed as the enemy. Carole knew that most judges were a lot more interested in the work of the horse and the rider than in grooming, but she also knew that a dirty horse or an unkempt outfit could distract a judge's attention from the things that mattered, like skill. These riders knew it, too. The entire stable area was a frenzy of activity.

Jean DeSoto was crouching in front of Topside, putting yet another coat of polish on his hooves. Dorothy stood in front of a dingy mirror, tucking strands of hair into a hairnet.

"Hi, Max," Carole said. "We're here!"

Max glanced at his watch. Carole was pleased to note that in spite of their detour in the Garden's confused hallways, they were on time. Max smiled with relief. Then he spotted Skye. The girls had discussed how to explain Skye to Max. Max certainly wouldn't know who the teenage actor was, so telling him about the meeting in the park was going to sound too weird. They'd decided to say he was the son of Marine Corps friends of Carole's father because Skye's father *was* in the Corps. So it was sort of the truth.

Skye shook hands with Max and Mrs. Reg. The girls were pleased with their story, until Dorothy turned around from the mirror. She took one look at Skye and her jaw dropped.

"Skye Ransom!" she said. "What are you doing here?"

Max looked puzzled. "Was your father in the Corps with his, too?" he asked Dorothy.

"No, Max," Dorothy said. "This is *Skye Ransom*."

"I know," Max said. "We were just introduced."

"I mean, it's *Skye Ransom*. Don't you know who he is?" Max's blank look answered the question. "He's a movie star, Max. He's the teen idol of today. Girls swoon over him."

Max turned to his students and raised an eyebrow quizzically.

"He's also a Marine Corps kid, like me, and he's trying to learn to ride for a movie role," Carole said. "We thought an afternoon at the horse show would help so we invited him along. He's wearing his riding clothes so he won't attract attention. It's okay, isn't it?" she asked.

"Of course it's okay," Dorothy said, speaking for Max. "But I don't think Skye here is going to get much attention this afternoon. *I* just heard a rumor that Princess Di is at the show!"

The girls and Skye exchanged glances and burst into laughter. The grown-ups would never understand. They didn't even try to explain.

"Time to get out of here, you guys," Dorothy said. "Mother and I have a lot of work to do. The afternoon program begins with a class of Working Hunter and then my event—the Open Jumper class. Go on out there and enjoy the show, okay?"

"I think the operative word here is 'go,'" Mrs. Reg said sensibly, aiming the group toward the door.

The girls wished Dorothy good luck and then left. Carole led the way. The girls, Skye, and the Regnerys walked back through the stable area, past the warm-up ring and the door to the arena. The program had begun and the first rider was already out on the course. The second rider waited tensely by the double doors.

Carole watched the rider waiting to go on. She wondered what must be going through the woman's head. She sat absolutely still on her horse. Her face was a study in stony concentration. She seemed to be controlling her breathing, taking long, deep breaths.

"Thirty seconds," a woman by the door told the rider. The rider only blinked acknowledgment.

There was applause from the audience. Carole could hear the first competitor's horse cantering toward the door. The door swung open to admit them.

"Smile!" the starter told the rider. The rider's entire face changed. All solemnity was gone. Her face became the picture of joy and confidence. She gave her horse an almost invisible signal and the horse sprang to life, as transformed as his rider. Together, they bounded out into the arena, ready for the ride of their lives. It almost took Carole's breath away.

Quickly, Carole stepped into the seating area. Max led the way to Dorothy's box. They filed into the seats and sat down quickly. They didn't want to distract the horse and rider on the course. Although a good show horse was accustomed to noise and motion in the audience, it could bother a horse's concentration, and the rider's score would suffer. Nobody wanted to be responsible for that.

Skye sat between Lisa and Carole. He watched intently as the rider worked the jumps.

"I don't look like that when I ride, do I?" Skye whispered.

"No, you don't," Carole said with a smile. "But if you watch closely, you'll learn."

He didn't take his eyes off the rider. It pleased Carole. She was sure he *would* learn. If only they had more time!

There were a lot of entrants in the Working Hunter class. Carole relaxed and enjoyed the show. She loved it—every minute of it. The shows she had been to were outdoor shows, and although horses were really meant to ride outdoors, the indoor arena somehow gave a kind of intimacy to the show and made her feel closer to the horses and riders. She could hear every beat of the horses' hooves. She could hear the squeak of the clean leather tack. Their ringside seats were even close enough to hear the riders talk to their horses as they passed by.

"The important thing in this event is form," Carole explained to Skye. "The jumps aren't particularly high, so just getting over them isn't hard. What's hard is doing it right. See, the horse has to keep an even pace and needs to jump smoothly. The instructions of the rider are really important. Notice the way this rider keeps taking off for the jump too close, so her horse has to slow down before jumping so he won't ram into it. She's also having trouble keeping him from speeding up right after the jump. But look at the way she sits at the canter. It's about perfect. You'll want to look like that."

Skye watched carefully. Carole was sure he was learning. It had been a good idea to bring him.

The first event lasted almost forty-five minutes, but it seemed to Carole that it was only about ten. She couldn't believe how fast it went. In between horses, Skye asked questions about the riders and what they'd done right or wrong. That gave the girls a chance to tell him all kinds of things they'd forgotten to mention when they were riding.

"Did you see that one's wrists?" Lisa said. "They were *all* wrong. No way they should drop like that. You hold them like this." She demonstrated.

After the Working Hunter event was finished, there was a delay in the show while one set of jumps was removed and another put up. Carole watched the workmen for a while and then her attention turned to the audience around her and across the arena from her.

A lot of the people there were riders or owners and seemed to know one another. For the most part, this was a horse-wise crowd. There were a lot of young riders in the audience, too. They were watching everything as eagerly as The Saddle Club.

Then there were people who seemed to be at the horse show for some reason other than horses. There were little kids who kept nagging their mothers for food and drinks. They dashed along the aisles of the enormous arena trying to catch up with souvenir hawkers.

There were other people, adults, who seemed to be more interested in being seen than in seeing. One woman in particular caught Carole's eye. She came in late. She strode through the entrance gate and stood as if waiting for applause. She was tall and slender and wore a flowing red cloak, which she removed dramatically, swinging it around like a bullfighter. Carole thought it was a good thing there were no bulls around. The woman marched to her box seats, her escort trailing behind her. She headed to the front row, directly across from Dorothy's box.

"Check her out! I think it's Big Red Riding-Hood," Stevie said, pointing at the woman.

Lisa nodded, laughing. "A lot of people are looking at her—probably think she's Princess Di!"

It could be true. The woman was doing everything she could to get attention. Before she sat down, she did the twirling act with her cloak one more time. Even in an arena that held thousands of spectators people were noticing her. She seemed to like that a lot.

In the arena, the jumps were assembled very carefully. It was a tricky course. The jumps were both wide and high. Even the best riders could have trouble with some of those, Carole thought. This course would require incredible skill and total concentration.

Across the way, Big Red Riding-Hood made a show of talking to one of the riders. Carole knew she was a rider because of the number pinned to her back. Even as they chatted, the woman continued swirling her coat. Then the rider walked back out of the arena into the stable area.

The tractors and trailers drove out of the ring. It was time for the Open Jumper class to begin. Carole felt a shudder of excitement. Now they'd see Dorothy ride! It was time to ignore Big Red Riding-Hood and focus on the horses and riders again.

"This is a very different event from the Working Hunter," Carole explained to Skye. "In this class, form doesn't matter at all. What matters is getting over the jumps and doing it fast. You get faulted for knocking jumps down or for taking too much time. It's a race against the clock and it's a very exciting event."

That proved to be true from the very first rider. His horse dashed around the course and leapt over the jumps. It was a real change after the comparatively genteel Working Hunter class. The man made it through the course without knocking down any jumps, but in spite of his efforts at speed, he exceeded the time allowed. The audience clapped for him, though. He'd put on quite a show.

The next rider did fine on time, but knocked down two jumps.

"Too bad," Carole said. "He won't make it into the top fifteen for the finals."

Then there were three more horses. Two went through the course without knocking down anything, though one had a time fault. The third horse was a beauty—a sleek gray warmblood who was obviously fired up for the competition. As his rider rode him around before beginning the course, the horse, who was named Roo, bucked all over the place.

"He's trying to throw her off!" Skye said.

"No, I don't think so," Carole told him. "If he wanted to throw her, he could probably do it. He's just full of vinegar and she knows it. This should be a good round."

It was, too, and it was funny as well. The horse never stopped bucking, but it didn't slow Roo one bit. He'd buck after each jump and he'd buck through each jump, whipping his legs out behind him. It seemed to lift him even higher.

Every time Roo bucked, his rider tapped him on the flank with her crop to remind him that there was work to do. Then he'd spring toward the next jump and buck his way over that. The whole audience was laughing as well as cheering when the two finished the course. They hadn't knocked down any jumps and they were within the time allowed.

"That was great!" Skye said. "I wish I could ride

like that!" Carole looked at him. For the first time, Carole saw real horse interest in him. It meant that he was beginning to think about riding as something he wanted to do instead of something he had to do. She smiled to herself. They'd make a rider out of Skye Ransom yet!

The next rider was the woman Big Red Riding-Hood had been talking to. When she rode out on her horse and greeted the judges, she also waved to her friend and her friend waved back. The horse was a mare named Pearl and she had a disappointing round. She knocked down two jumps and refused a third. By the time they finished the course, it was clear they'd be eliminated. The rider was disappointed, of course, but the look on Big Red Riding-Hood's face, even from across the arena, was clear. It was disgust. She stood up to leave.

Carole would have kept watching her except that the next rider was Dorothy. Carole slid her hands under the program that lay on her lap and crossed her fingers. She knew that good riders were the result of hard work and training, not luck, but luck couldn't hurt. She glanced over at Lisa. Lisa's fingers were crossed, too.

Topside and Dorothy entered the arena, and the Pine Hollow group applauded loudly when Dorothy's name was announced. She circled the arena to warm up and then, when Topside was ready, they began the course.

Topside was completely tuned for this round. He raced to the first jump and sailed over it so easily that the audience said "Oooh!" His coat gleamed under the bright lights from the ceiling and shimmered as his muscles rippled. He was beautiful and elegant and he was going to win!

Dorothy changed directions to return to the far end of the arena. There was a triple jump combination that had already been knocked down by several of the horses. Topside flew over all three of the jumps almost as if they weren't there. He swished his tail proudly after each jump.

Carole could barely swallow because of the thrill of Topside's beautiful performance.

Dorothy brought Topside straight along the far side of the ring, toward the tricky double combination. He cleared the first jump with more than a foot to spare.

The woman with the red cape turned around.

Topside neared the second jump of the combination.

The woman picked up her red cape.

Dorothy leaned forward, rose in the saddle, and signaled Topside to jump.

The woman grabbed her cape angrily and swirled it around.

Topside rose in the air.

At that instant his eye caught the sudden flash of movement close by.

Topside panicked. He bucked in midair and landed

stiff-legged. Then he reared! Dorothy was tossed out of the saddle like a handful of straw. She landed hard on her back, her head striking the jump they'd just cleared. She rolled halfway over and then she lay limp and motionless.

Carole was vaguely aware of the screams of fear, concern, and anger from the audience, but she was mostly aware of the still presence of Dorothy DeSoto. Without even thinking, Carole scrambled over the fence in front of her yard and into the arena. Max was right behind her. Dozens of people from the audience and the backstage area ran to help Dorothy.

Carole, eager to do something helpful, took hold of Topside's reins and checked him over. He seemed all right, but a little skittish, as if something else could set him off again. She walked him around the arena to calm him. It would be reassuring to the horse to do something so normal. She wished somebody could do something to reassure her!

As they reached the far end of the arena, Carole looked up toward the crowd. The people were standing still, watching Dorothy with great concern. The only movement, in fact, was a blur of bright red, marching out of the arena.

"IT'S IMPORTANT FOR us to do this, you know," Carole said to her friends the next morning. They stood together on the sidewalk outside of the riding stable. "Just because Dorothy got hurt in a riding accident doesn't mean everybody gets hurt in riding accidents. We are good riders. We love horses. We *should* do this."

Stevie looked at her friend. In a way, Carole was absolutely right. As it was important for a rider who had been thrown to get back on a horse, it was important for three girls who had witnessed a riding accident to get back in the saddle. She didn't want her nerves to beat her.

"You're right," she said. "And besides, Skye needs us."

"Speaking of Skye, where is he?" Lisa asked. "He

shot out of the horse show right after Dorothy fell. Do
you suppose . . . ?"

"I think he had to get to the movie set," Stevie
said. She didn't want to consider the fact that Skye
might have been more frightened than they were.

"I think he was scared," Lisa said. "I was, that's for
sure."

It *had* been scary. Stevie and Lisa had gone to Dorothy and waited with her until the ambulance had arrived. One man in the audience had tried to help
Dorothy sit up until Stevie stopped him.

"She might have hurt her back!" Stevie had told
the man sternly. She knew that in the case of back
injuries, it could be dangerous to move a patient. She
had learned something useful from her Health class
after all.

Dorothy had thanked Stevie for her concern but
said she thought it was a broken rib or two.

"I've had enough of those," she'd said. "I'll be back
in the saddle in a couple of weeks." Nevertheless, Dorothy had followed Stevie's advice and remained still
until the paramedics shifted her to the stretcher.

Max had gone to the hospital with Jean DeSoto.
Mrs. Reg and the girls had untacked Topside, fed and
watered him, and returned to Dorothy's house to wait.

Max and Mrs. DeSoto hadn't returned until late.
They'd spent hours in the emergency room with Dorothy. Max swore that they'd x-rayed every inch of Doro-

thy's body. Although a preliminary reading showed no immediate danger to Dorothy, nobody would be able to give a thorough reading until the morning. In the meantime, Dorothy was heavily sedated and sleeping soundly.

Since there wasn't anything they could do to help and since they'd made a deal with Skye to meet at the stable early in the morning, the girls had left the house early and now stood nervously in front of the city stable.

"You know, all my life, when something was going wrong, the one thing I could count on being right was horseback riding," Carole said. "Now that horseback riding is what's gone wrong, I don't know how to handle it."

"With horseback riding," Lisa said sensibly. "Let's go."

Lisa climbed the steps and walked up to the desk to arrange for the horses.

Stevie was ready first. While Lisa and Carole finished pulling on their boots, Stevie paced in front of the window, looking out to see if Skye would arrive, but there wasn't any sign of him. When a half hour had passed and he still hadn't shown up, the girls realized that he wasn't going to show up.

"That's his problem," Stevie said to Lisa and Carole. "Let's not make it ours. Let's go."

The three of them tightened up their horses' girths, mounted up, and headed for the park.

It was still early in the morning, much earlier than they had ridden on the previous days. There were a few joggers and some people walking their dogs, but aside from that, The Saddle Club had the park to themselves. The horses seemed eager to enjoy the early-morning ride. Stevie was riding a pinto who was full of spirit. The horse's enthusiasm was positively infectious.

Within a few minutes, the girls were all trotting happily along the bridle path around the city's scenic reservoir. The park was ringed by tall apartment buildings, providing a dramatic background to the trees and bushes.

"Let's play merry-go-round," Lisa suggested. It was a game they could play when they could ride three abreast. They alternated leading, but the leader could never be more than a half a horse-length ahead of the others. It was a game that required them to control their gaits very carefully. The girls had had a lot of practice in precision riding when they'd formed a three-person drill team. This was a challenge, though, and they all had fun.

Stevie's horse was giving her trouble and she loved it. He was so full of spirit that he always wanted to be the leader. It took a lot of concentration to get him to slow down, just a bit, to let Lisa's horse take the lead when it was her turn.

After merry-go-ground, they tried follow-the-leader. That was one of Stevie's favorite games. When she was the leader, she dreamed up some of the kookiest ideas. Not only did she drop her stirrups, but she also made her friends drop their reins for a few seconds! They complained, but she knew they liked it.

Stevie couldn't believe how fast the hour went. When Carole pointed out that it was time to go back to the stable, Stevie looked at her watch three times.

"Maybe Skye will be there waiting for us when we get back," Lisa said.

Maybe he would be, Stevie thought. It was possible that he'd just overslept. Possible, she decided, but not probable. What was probable was that Skye was too frightened to continue riding.

One phone call confirmed it. Stevie was elected to call Skye. They didn't know where he was staying, but they reached his manager's office. Stevie couldn't convince the secretary that she wasn't just another one of Skye's adoring fans. However, when she asked the woman where the manager was, his secretary said he was involved in a script conference—something about cutting out the horseback-riding scene in the movie Skye was filming.

"We blew it," Stevie said, turning to her friends after she'd hung up the phone. "We tried to show him how wonderful riding could be and it looks like all we succeeded in doing was scaring him away for good!"

"We *did* try," Lisa said sadly. "We did the best we could. It's not our fault that he's scared."

"That's true," Carole agreed. "But what really

bothers me is the idea that Skye might never ride again. Think what he'll be missing!"

Stevie realized that Carole was right. She thought about how much fun they'd just had playing games on horseback during their early-morning ride. It wouldn't be fair to let anybody miss that. They just had to find him and get him back to his riding lessons.

"This sounds like a job for The Saddle Club, don't you think?" Stevie said. Lisa and Carole agreed with her about that.

WHEN THE GIRLS got back to Dorothy's, they found Max and Mrs. Reg sitting in Dorothy's living room. They were drinking coffee and talking quietly. As soon as they walked in, Lisa knew something bad was up—and the bad thing had to be about Dorothy.

"What did the X rays show?" Lisa asked.

Max and Mrs. Reg invited the girls to sit down. Max took a deep breath and began speaking.

"Dorothy's going to be okay," he said. "That's the good news. She was right that she had a broken rib. In fact, she has three, but that's not the problem. The problem is that she has something called a compression fracture in one of her vertebrae—those are the bones of her spine. It will heal. It should heal completely, actually, and Dorothy will be able to live an almost completely normal life. This is all very good news. The bad news is that the doctor said if Dorothy ever were to reinjure her back, and another riding accident could do it easily, she'd be much more likely to damage her spinal cord, and that could put her in a wheelchair for life."

The girls looked at one another. The implication was sinking in.

Max continued. "What this means is that Dorothy DeSoto can never ride in competition again."

9

CAROLE HAD DECIDED a long time ago that horses were what she wanted to do with her life. She hadn't decided yet whether she wanted to raise them, train them, or heal them, but she knew she would always want to ride them. She could not imagine what her life would be like if that were taken away from her.

She followed Stevie and Lisa along the hallway of the hospital where Dorothy was recovering from her accident. Hospitals were good at helping people's bodies recover from accidents, but what could a hospital do about somebody's spirit, she wondered. How could Dorothy's body heal, how could the broken bone in her back mend, when her heart must be broken? And, even more immediately, what could Carole do or say to help? She walked in silent thought.

"Six forty-two, forty-four . . . and here's forty-six,"

Stevie announced, peering into the strange room. Then she stepped in. Lisa followed after her.

Carole stood in the hallway, waiting for her own courage. Hospitals were difficult for her. She remembered all too vividly her visits with her mother before she had died. But this was nothing like that. Dorothy was going to make a full recovery. She'd walk, laugh, love, even run again. But she'd never ride in competition again. *Never.* The word kept repeating itself to Carole.

Stevie broke into Carole's thoughts by bouncing out of Dorothy's room and into the hallway. "Hey, get in here!" she said cheerfully. "Dorothy's wondering if you want to see her!" From anybody but Stevie or Lisa, Carole might have been annoyed at the insistence. But her friends cared enough about her to know exactly how she was feeling and what she was thinking right then. And they knew that thinking sad thoughts wasn't going to help anything.

She walked slowly into the room and pulled back the curtain that circled Dorothy's bed.

Dorothy didn't look so bad. She lay flat on her back with her arms at her sides. There was an IV in one arm, and a bandage on her forehead. She had a black eye. More important, however, there was a smile on her face.

Carole smiled back.

"I look great, don't I?" Dorothy teased.

"You look wonderful," Carole told her sincerely.

"And you look a lot better than you did day before yesterday when poor Topside freaked. Does it hurt?"

"It hurts some," Dorothy told her truthfully. "If I can keep from moving at all, I'm better off. But that's not what you meant by hurt, is it?"

Carole looked down and shook her head. She should have known that Dorothy would understand what she was really asking.

"Yes, it hurts," Dorothy said. "I've ridden in hundreds of competitions, put on lots of demonstrations, traveled all over the world—as a rider. That's gone. Ended. It hurts."

Carole sat down on a chair by the bed and took one of Dorothy's hands. It was all she could think of to comfort her friend. Dorothy squeezed her hand in thanks.

"But look, Carole, girls, I was a professional. I *am* a professional. My profession has risks and I've always known what they are. There are a lot of promising riders who get hurt and bounced out of the field at your age. That didn't happen to me. I was lucky, really. I've been riding professionally for more than fifteen years. They've been wonderful years, but they've taken their toll, too."

She paused to take a sip of water, then continued. "Sometimes I travel so much, I don't know where I am or what language I should be speaking. I hate myself sometimes for thinking more about my colleagues as my competition than as my friends. There have been days when I've thought about my riding as a job, just a job, something I *had* to do because it was the only thing I *could* do. Those were bad days. Now they are behind me. So I will look on the bright side. I can still work with horses. I will probably be able to ride for pleasure. I can train horses, I can take care of them. I can do all kinds of things. I just can't compete. It could be worse. If Topside had gotten spooked half a second earlier, we might have landed *on* the jump, Topside could have gotten hurt, and I might have been hurt worse."

"Or less," Carole added.

"Maybe," Dorothy said. "But there's no point analyzing what might have been. What I've got here is a case of what *is*, not what *if*."

It was so simple, and so complicated.

"More flowers, Miss DeSoto," a young man announced, walking into the room. Carole had been so concerned with Dorothy that she hadn't even noticed the fact that the reason the room seemed so small was because it was packed full of flowers.

"It's embarrassing," Dorothy confessed to the girls. "I never saw so many flowers in one place! See who it's from, will you?"

Lisa took the card from the flowers, a cheery arrangement of bright summer blossoms, and, as she read, the surprise showed in her eyes.

"It's from Skye Ransom!" she said.

"Oh, how nice!" Dorothy said. "And won't the

young nurses here be jealous!" She laughed. "You were riding with him yesterday morning, weren't you? How is he doing with his lessons?"

"He's not," Carole said. "He disappeared after your accident and he didn't show up for the lesson yesterday. We talked to his manager's secretary and it sounded like he got completely freaked. We want to talk to him, but we don't know where to find him."

"Oh, that's terrible," Dorothy said. "Just because I had an accident doesn't mean he shouldn't ride. There must be a way you can get hold of him . . ." She wrinkled her forehead to think. "Maybe call the florist?"

Lisa looked at the tag on the arrangement. "Bingo!" she announced. "The flowers come from the florist at the Plaza Hotel. I bet that's where he's staying."

"Well, then you must go there," Dorothy said. "If he's staying there, you can at least leave a message for him."

"But we don't want to leave you," Lisa said. "We just got here."

"It's okay," Dorothy assured her. "Getting Skye back to riding is important. And from what I've seen of the way you girls work, it's a job for The Saddle Club. Go to it!"

The girls grinned at one another. "Okay," Carole agreed.

"But we're just doing this for you," Lisa said.

"Sure, sure," Dorothy said. "I know, just to please me, you'll sacrifice your precious time in New York to find this poor, ugly, uninteresting dweeb at the Plaza so you can talk horses with him, right?"

Laughing, the girls all gave Dorothy a little hand squeeze, and promised to come back for another visit soon and to report progress on the new Saddle Club project: Operation Skye Ransom.

"NEW YORK IS unbelievable," Stevie said a half hour later as they emerged from a subway. Carole gazed at street signs, Lisa stared at a map, and Stevie thought out loud. "No matter how many people you ask for directions, you always get a different answer! And when you look at the map, Lisa, you always say they're *all* right!"

"If this is Central Park," Lisa said, pointing behind her, "then the Plaza Hotel is—"

"There it is!" Carole said. "I recognize it from movies. Look at all the limos in front of it!"

Stevie and Lisa looked where she was pointing. Stevie knew she was right. She recognized it, too. The threesome waited for the lights to change so they could cross the streets, and then made their way into the lobby of the world-famous hotel.

That was when they realized they didn't have the slightest idea how to proceed.

"We ask for him at the desk," Lisa suggested. It seemed simple enough. Since Lisa was the oldest of them, they decided she should do it. Stevie and Carole stood back and tried to look inconspicuous. They thought it could take Lisa quite a while to get the information. It didn't take any time at all. Lisa was back to them within seconds.

"No way," she said. "The clerk was really nasty. Said they don't give out guests' room numbers—especially to *kids*. I guess we're not the first of Skye's fans to figure out that he's staying here."

"But we're not fans," Stevie said. "I mean, we are, but we're here to help him. Did you tell the clerk that?"

"I got the impression that the last girl who'd asked for his room number tried to convince the guy she was his sister—then his aunt. Believe me, they've probably heard it all."

"So what are we going to do?" Carole asked.

"We'll have to wait for him," Stevie said. "We'll go park ourselves near the elevators and he's bound to come through sometime. And when that time comes, we'll be here."

"I think this may be a dumb idea," Lisa said.

"It may be," Stevie conceded, "but it's all we've got."

The girls followed the path through the lobby, which led to the elevator bank. There was an upholstered banquette there. They planted themselves on it and waited.

"I feel dumb," Lisa said. "I mean, this is so *obvious*.

The clerk I talked to keeps looking over his desk at us."

"Maybe we should each buy a newspaper to read," Stevie suggested. "Then, like in the movies, we can poke holes in it to peep through. Nobody will ever notice!"

"Nobody except the house detective over there," Lisa said. She gestured toward a man in a brown suit who had been standing by the door and was clearly watching the girls. "But then, maybe we should do it. He probably hasn't had a good laugh for a long—"

"There he is!" Stevie said, jumping up.

"Skye?" Lisa asked excitedly.

"No, Frank Nelson. Skye's manager," Stevie told her, starting to run. Mr. Nelson was almost out the door before the girls caught him.

He had a terribly worried look on his face and, at first, was not at all interested in talking to the girls.

"It's over, don't you see?" he said in exasperation. "You and your bright ideas. You got him scared to death. He's never going to ride again. We've lost this deal—in the middle of filming—and we're going to have a giant lawsuit on our hands, all thanks to—"

"But that's the thing!" Stevie interrupted. "It's not our fault and we want to help."

"Big help!" Mr. Nelson snorted. "Sure, tell him how your friend got all banged up and will never ride again. According to the papers, it's a lucky thing she'll ever walk!"

Stevie knew that both Mr. Nelson and Skye were looking at the whole situation upside down. She was sure that if they could talk to Skye they could convince him to start riding again. And if they didn't, he'd be missing the opportunity to do one of the most wonderful things there was—horseback riding.

"You've *got* to let us see him!" she said, feeling almost desperate.

"I *don't* have to let you do anything," Mr. Nelson responded, more than a little irritated. "And right now, I'm on my way to a lawyer's office. You girls can't possibly understand, but there's a lot at stake here!"

"That's where you're wrong, Mr. Nelson," Stevie said. "We do understand that there's a lot at stake. It's just that what you think is at stake and what we think is at stake are two different things."

He looked at her, interested for the first time.

"Besides," Stevie said, ready for her final attack. "What have you got to lose?"

"Suite fourteen-oh-one," he said. "Knock on the door like *Dragnet*—you know, dum-de-dum-dum. He'll open it. He'll know I sent you."

10

DUM-DE-DUM-*dum*.

Dum-de-dum-dum-dah!

The door opened. There was Skye Ransom, wearing jeans and a polo shirt, with bare feet and tousled hair.

"What are you doing here?" he demanded.

"Mr. Nelson said it was okay," Lisa began. "We just wanted to talk to you."

He looked at the three girls standing in the hallway for a moment. He started to speak, first with anger crossing his face, then all emotion hidden behind his actor's mask. Finally, he said simply, "Come in."

At first, Lisa was almost overwhelmed by the suite. It was elegant and opulent. It had a large living room—much bigger than the one in her parents' house, and much fancier, too. At one end of it, there was a desk with a computer and telephone. A woman sat and worked at the keyboard.

"That's Frank's secretary," Skye said, introducing them quickly. "So what do you want to talk about?" he challenged them.

"Horses," Stevie said, meeting the problem head-on. "Mr. Nelson says you don't want to ride any more and you're trying to get out of doing the movie."

"So what?" he asked. "I'm not real interested in ending up in the hospital like you friend. She's in bad shape!"

It was what Lisa had expected him to say, but she was still surprised to hear the deep fear in his voice. Without even thinking, she blurted, "Dorothy's in better shape than you are!"

Skye looked at her, stunned. "She's in the hospital with a broken neck, practically. Her career is over, bang, just like that! Are you saying that's better off than I am?"

His fear gave Lisa the strength she needed. "Maybe her career as a competitive rider *is* over, but she's got lots of options in front of her and she's not afraid. From what I hear, it's possible that this could end your career, too—and you *are* afraid. It may look like you're both in the same boat, with your careers in trouble, but at least Dorothy knows what's what.

"We just came from visiting her. She's the bravest and strongest person I ever met. If you don't believe us that you're making a mistake, you should believe her. She's the one who told us to come get you and make you go back to riding!"

Both Stevie and Carole looked at Lisa. She knew she'd surprised them as much as she'd surprised Skye and herself. Lisa was usually the shy, mild-mannered one who did exactly what everybody expected of her and never made any waves, but this was too important. She just couldn't stand by and let Skye ruin his career, and his life, by being afraid to ride.

"She's right, you know," Stevie added.

"Yeah," Carole finished, making it a unanimous vote.

Skye was skeptical. "Are you telling me that just seeing your poor friend in the hospital is going to make me want to hop back on a horse?"

"No," Lisa said. "I don't think that for a minute. But I think that if, after seeing Dorothy, you still decide not to ride, at least you will have made an informed decision instead of an emotional one." For a moment, she was afraid that she'd sounded an awful lot like the report she'd had to write on last year's election, but Skye didn't seem to notice.

"Okay," he agreed. "We'll go to the hospital." He reached for his socks and sneakers, carelessly tossed on the floor by the sofa. Lisa found it very comforting to know that underneath it all, Skye Ransom was very normal.

THIS TIME, THE girls weren't so nervous walking along the hallway of the hospital. The nurses tried to tell the four of them that only three visitors at a time were allowed, but when they saw that one of them was Skye Ransom, all of a sudden there was no problem. Lisa was relieved about that. She didn't want any of them to miss this visit.

The girls rushed to the bedside to greet Dorothy, but Skye hung back by the door. "Don't be shy now," Dorothy said, greeting Skye. "I'm not so bad, am I?" she asked, smiling behind her black eye.

"Well, *I* think you'd be a good model for the makeup crew for the next *Rocky* movie," Stevie joked, trying to lighten the tension in the room. "I love the black eye!"

"It doesn't hurt," Dorothy said. "The doctor said it's the result of head trauma. Doesn't that sound fancy?"

Skye finally smiled. "That sounds like something you need a psychiatrist for!" he joked.

"Oh, they sent one of those in here, too," Dorothy said. "And when he went out, he felt much better. See, he was having this problem with the nursing staff, and I just told him that—"

"You're joking," Skye said.

"Only a little," Dorothy confessed. "See, the common wisdom is that I'm supposed to be a basket case. But I'm not. I'm simply recognizing what the facts are."

"But the facts are *awful,*" Skye reminded her.

"Come, sit down, and let's talk," Dorothy said to Skye. He pulled a chair up to her bedside and sat down. "You and I have a lot in common," she began. "We're both performers and, though in different ways, we're both competitors."

Skye seemed suddenly a lot more interested than he had been. Lisa could tell that Dorothy had struck a chord.

"And we both know there are risks. Mine are obvious. Yours not so obvious, but they're there. You could do a lousy movie and no matter how good *you* are, the movie bombs and your reputation goes sour. Or you could do a poor job on a good film and suddenly nobody wants to take a chance on you. Or you could get into a lot of legal trouble with a production company and nobody will touch you with a ten-foot pole."

"I know these things," Skye said.

"I know you do. You also know that you could be doing a stunt and, wham, something goes wrong, and you've got a broken arm, a concussion, a cut, or what I have: a compression fracture of a vertebral body."

"I don't do dangerous stunts," he said.

"Or these things could happen to you crossing the street or climbing out of a bathtub! The point is that being alive is risky. If you're going to let yourself be held hostage to your fears, you might as well climb into that empty hospital bed there, pull the sheets up, and stay there for the rest of your life. No, on second thought, even that's too dangerous—wait until you try the food here!"

Skye laughed in spite of himself. "I think you're telling me to climb back on the horse, aren't you? I've heard that one before." He glanced at the girls.

"Well, they're right. So what if you fall off. You fell off the other day, didn't you? What got hurt?"

"I've got a bruise—"

"And that's not all," Dorothy said gently.

Skye looked down at the floor, then confessed, "Well, I guess I've always thought I could do anything and everything, and nobody ever told me different, except that horse and Topside. Those horses showed me that riding is very risky."

"Who cares what the horse thinks?" Dorothy asked. "I'm much more concerned with what Skye thinks."

"Skye thinks he's a lousy rider," Skye told her. "And being a lousy rider is dangerous."

"Skye's right about that. And there's only one cure for being a lousy rider and that's practice."

Skye sat back in the chair and crossed his arms over his chest. A young nurse came into the room and adjusted Dorothy's IV. An intern came in and took her temperature and checked her pulse. A nursing student came in to adjust the blankets on her bed. Skye sat deep in thought through this flurry of activity.

"I think the word's gotten around that Skye Ransom is in my room," Dorothy whispered, grinning impishly. "I haven't had this much attention since I arrived. Next thing you know, the nutritionist is going to want to know how I liked the ravioli I had for lunch yesterday."

The girls giggled. Being with Skye Ransom had some very funny aspects.

"Ah! Miss DeSoto!" An older woman appeared at the door. "The nutrition department wants to welcome you to our hospital and let you know that we'll—"

Dorothy shot a dirty look at the girls, who were about to explode with laughter. They stifled it politely, while Dorothy assured the woman that the ravioli had been fine.

"Skye, I think you're going to have to move along before they start drawing blood samples just to get a look at you!"

He laughed. "I'm sorry. I'm causing you a lot of trouble. I'm causing Lisa and Carole and Stevie a lot of trouble. And then there's my manager and the production company and the Hollywood people." He blew out a big breath and shook his head. "I'm being a jerk. I've been a jerk from the start. I'm the one who lied about being able to ride, so it's not fair to all these other people to put them to a lot of trouble because I lied." He looked at Lisa. "How far away am I? If I can ride with you this afternoon for a couple of hours, do you think I'll be able to pull it off on camera?"

Lisa looked at Carole and Stevie. They nodded. "It won't be easy," she said. "But you're a good student and a determined one. It's certainly worth a try. And we're willing to help."

"You've been such a big help already," Skye said. He wrinkled his brow in thought. "I'll ride with you today on one condition."

"And what's that?" Lisa asked, glancing at her friends with a worried expression.

Skye grinned. "That you'll ride with me tomorrow."

"But tomorrow's your shoot, isn't it?" Stevie asked. "The big riding scene in the movie?"

"That's what I mean," he said. "You've *got* to be there! I can't see myself riding in front of a camera without Lisa to pick me up off the ground when I fall, Carole to tell me absolutely everything there is to know about horses, and Stevie to make a joke about it. Will you be there? As extras? Can you do it?"

They assured him they could!

11

EVEN MAX TURNED out to watch the filming. He and Mrs. Reg were given folding chairs and a spot in the shade.

The scene was being filmed in a wooded area of Staten Island, another part of New York City. It was supposed to look as if it were Central Park, but being in a more remote section of the city gave the crew more flexibility in the filming.

Skye set up the scene for them: His character was supposed to have a big crush on a girl named Molly. This Molly was a horseback rider, so he wanted to impress her, even though her father didn't like him. The trouble was that his character, Brad, wasn't all that good a rider. His horse would get out of control, start running away, and Molly would come to his rescue.

"Sounds like real life, doesn't it?" Skye asked, winking at Lisa.

She smiled back at him. "Should be easy enough, except that everybody knows the hardest thing in the world is to know what you're doing and to look like you don't."

Skye laughed. "That's why I'm glad you three are here."

They were glad, too.

It hadn't been easy getting there, either. For one thing, the scene hadn't called for extras. The director wasn't enthusiastic about letting them into the film. Finally, Skye had just plain asked that they be allowed to do it as a special favor to him, explaining that The Saddle Club had been extremely helpful in preparing him to do the scene. The director had agreed.

Then, there had been the matter of horses for them. The director had arranged for four horses, two each for Skye and his costar. The girls could certainly use the backups, for all the riding they were doing, but that left one of them on foot.

It had taken Max to come up with a solution to that. He pointed out that there was an excellent horse at their disposal who would otherwise spend another day cooped up in the overcrowded stable area of Madison Square Garden, just waiting for somebody to move him someplace. Stevie was riding Topside.

As soon as she mounted him, Stevie knew that Topside was every bit as special as she'd hoped. He had wonderful strength and was very responsive. She leaned forward in the saddle and patted his neck to put him at ease. He looked back over his shoulder and nodded. Stevie could have sworn he was trying to put *her* at ease, but that, of course, was impossible.

While the director worked on placing the cameras, The Saddle Club took time to ride around the grounds where the filming would take place.

And every time Skye had a free minute, he came out of his personal trailer and joined them for last-minute refresher lessons.

"*How* do I get him to canter?" he asked Carole.

"*Her, her,*" Stevie reminded him. "Not that it matters, really, except to her, of course, but you're riding a mare, and her name is Roulette. She's a bay, just like Topside. That's what we call the color when a horse is basically brown, but—"

"Very interesting," he said, hiding a smile, "but how do I get *her* to canter?"

Carole spoke up. "You get her to trot and then you move your outside foot—that's the one away from the direction you're turning—back and touch her behind the girth. She'll probably respond immediately."

"I'll try it now," he said. He mounted Roulette.

Lisa rode with him to make sure it went smoothly. They trotted. His posting was all right. It didn't look perfect, but it looked good enough to pass for somebody who wasn't very good at posting.

"Nice," she said, to build his confidence. He smiled at her again. Lisa reflected that she was almost getting used to being with Skye Ransom. Almost. Her knees still buckled every time he smiled at her.

"Now," she said. She waited until Skye got Roulette to canter before giving her own horse the instruction. Just the sight of another horse cantering could be enough to get Roulette going, and she wanted it to be Skye's victory. Her horse caught up to Skye's and they cantered together.

"Try sitting deeper in the saddle," she said. "That way, you can rock with the gait more easily and not flap around so much. See, it's really a sliding motion. Pretend you're on a merry-go-round."

"Do they put sacks of potatoes on merry-go-rounds?" he asked.

"No, but then, you're no sack of potatoes."

"And I'm no Dorothy DeSoto, either."

"Neither am I," Lisa said.

Skye looked at her as if understanding for the first time that there was a big difference among riders—even skilled riders. "Thanks," he said, and she knew he meant it.

She had him bring his horse to a trot and then canter again. He didn't have any trouble doing it on his own, but the second Lisa's horse started cantering, Roulette did it, too. Skye just couldn't hold her back. Lisa wished there was more time to help him control his horse, but they had to stop practicing. The worst thing would be to overtire Skye's horse before the big scene.

The director waved to Skye. It was time for him to do something, so he left the girls where they were.

"This is so slow!" Stevie complained. "I thought we'd be in front of cameras all day, but I haven't even heard the word 'Action!'"

"Okay, girls, come on over here," the director's assistant called to them.

Lisa pasted on a smile, ready for her moment of glory in front of the cameras.

"Yours is over there," he said. They turned to see what he meant, ready for their great performance. That wasn't what he meant at all. It was lunchtime!

Lunch turned out to be dry cold cuts. It wasn't the sort of glamour meal that they'd been expecting. There was better food in the refrigerator of Skye's limousine!

"Is this the life of a movie star or what?" Stevie asked, looking at a hard piece of salami. "I think I'd prefer the hospital ravioli!"

"Hi, girls," an unfamiliar voice greeted them. Lisa turned to find herself face-to-face with the girl who was playing Molly. Lisa had the feeling she was supposed to know her name. The actress's face was vaguely familiar, but when Lisa, Stevie, and Carole introduced themselves, the girl didn't offer her name.

"I understand you're these super riders," she gushed, batting her eyelashes. "Isn't it a drag when you're a good rider and you have to work with somebody who doesn't know the first thing about riding?"

She didn't fool Lisa, Stevie, or Carole for one second. They recognized right away that "Molly" was trying to make Skye look bad. She wanted The Saddle Club to tell her what a bad rider he was.

"It can be awful," Stevie said. Molly's eyes lit up. "But on the other hand, you're lucky here because you've got Skye and you've got us, so if you get into trouble, we'll be glad to help you."

Molly smiled sweetly, but there was nothing sweet in the look she gave Stevie. "See you later," she said.

"What a creep!" Stevie said when she thought Molly was out of earshot.

"Yeah, a real jerk," Carole agreed. "Now we've *got* to make him look good."

"He's doing okay," Lisa said. "We were working on cantering and he'll pass. He's not great, but at least he's not scared anymore. Or, if he is, he's hiding it, and since he's such a good actor, that's about the same thing."

A bell rang then. The girls had been told that when the bell rang, it was time for the filming to begin. Quickly, they disposed of the remains of their unappetizing lunch, gulped final swallows of juice, donned their hats, mounted their horses, and headed for the cameras, ready to be discovered.

AT FIRST, IT didn't go well at all. The revised script called for Stevie, Lisa, and Carole to pass in front of the camera just to give the impression that there were other riders around. This wasn't hard. The first time they did it, the director gave them a "thumbs up" to show approval, then turned his attention right away to the heart of the scene.

"Molly! Molly!" Skye called out. It was his first line. Roulette began trotting.

Molly looked over her shoulder. "It's over between us, Brad, don't you understand?" She began cantering.

"Just because your father—" Skye couldn't finish his line. Roulette broke into a canter, chasing after Molly's horse. Roulette wasn't supposed to canter until after Skye finished his line.

"Cut!"

Everybody returned to their starting places.

"Action!"

The girls walked their horses in front of the camera. Thumbs up. So far, so good.

"Molly! Molly!" Roulette broke into a canter.

"Cut!"

Again.

Skye was having a really bad time controlling Roulette. Stevie noticed that the horse was just very eager to keep up with the horse Molly was riding, and Skye simply wasn't a good enough rider to make her do what he wanted. It wasn't the sort of riding technique they could teach him in a few lessons, and the lack of knowledge was showing.

"Action!"

The girls walked in front of the camera. Thumbs up.

Skye didn't even have a chance to deliver his first line that time. Roulette just took off. Stevie was watching Skye, but as he passed Molly, the actress drew Stevie's attention. There was no mistaking the look on the girl's face. It was a sneer of triumph. It was clear that Molly was trying to make Skye look bad. Stevie had no idea why that was so, but she wasn't going to let it happen. She and her friends had worked too hard to have Skye fail.

"Take five!" the director called out disgustedly. He was as tired of the scene as everybody else was.

The cast collected by the buffet table, where sodas had been laid out for them.

"I'm going to kill her," Skye hissed to The Saddle Club under his breath.

"Roulette?" Carole asked with concern.

"Oh, no!" Skye said. "She can't help herself and I can't keep her from doing it. No, the one I want to kill is Molly. Every time I get near her horse the way the script says, she clicks her tongue in her cheek. It's too quiet for the microphones to pick it up, but Roulette hears it all right and takes off. Molly is trying to make me look like an idiot—and she's succeeding! She's still sore that I got this part. She wanted her boyfriend to do it. This is probably her way of getting back at me."

"It's true that a lot of horses will recognize tongue

clucking as a signal to speed up," Carole said, frowning thoughtfully. "Also, mares can be feisty and a little unpredictable sometimes. This may be one of those times for Roulette. There isn't much you can do about it, except hold tight on the reins."

Skye took a soda. "I've been trying that. My hands are all sore. This horse has the best of me. I knew she'd be trouble from the time I first mounted her. I tried to get my costar to switch horses, but it's like she *knew* I'd have trouble with Roulette."

Stevie was steaming. "This is sabotage!" she hissed. "That jerk needs to be taught a lesson. I think I saw a nettle bush back in the woods. The four of us can grab her and dump her in there."

Skye laughed. "Great idea. I don't think the director will go for it, though."

"There's got to be a way," Stevie said stubbornly.

Stevie looked over to where the five horses were tied up under the shade of an elm tree. They looked so peaceful. Roulette and Topside were off to one side. The two bay horses looked a lot alike. As they stood there, sipping gently at their water, it was hard to tell that one was a skittish mare and the other was a championship Thoroughbred gelding. Very hard.

"I think I have the answer," Stevie said.

"ACTION!"

The three girls walked their horses in front of the camera. Thumbs up.

"Molly! Molly!" Skye trotted toward his costar.

"It's over between us, Brad, don't you understand?" Molly asked.

From where the girls waited, off-camera, they saw her cluck her tongue. It didn't faze Topside. Skye maintained an even trot. Molly clucked again.

"That's your cue, Molly!" the director called. "You're supposed to be cantering now!"

"Oh," she said weakly. She'd been so busy trying to make Skye look bad that she'd missed her own cue.

The girls exchanged glances and smirked to themselves. Skye just looked at Molly sympathetically. "Sometimes it's a little tricky controlling a horse, isn't it?" he asked. She sneered in response.

Again, the path was prepared, the cameras shifted back to their starting position. The girls returned to their starting places.

"Action!"

It went perfectly. Topside performed like a trouper.

"Just because your father can't accept me, doesn't mean we can't love each other!" Brad said clearly, declaring his love for Molly. At that moment, as planned, Topside broke into a canter. Topside almost seemed to sense Skye's discomfort and, when Skye's weight became unbalanced, Topside shifted his step to come under his rider.

They cantered around a bend in the path, disappearing into the woods.

"Cut!" the director said. There was an entirely different tone to his voice this time. It was joy, it was relief.

In a few moments, Skye and Molly reappeared down the path.

"Okay this time?" Skye asked.

"It was fine," the director said. "Now let's finish up and go home for the day."

The rest of the scene was easy. It was all dialogue and was going to be done at a walk, using close-ups. A complete nonrider could have done it. The tricky part was done and Skye had succeeded. So had Topside, and nobody was any the wiser!

The girls were allowed to wait and watch from behind the barriers. They joined Max and Mrs. Reg.

"Have you taken care of the horses?" Max asked. The girls nodded and laughed. It was just like Max to worry about the horses before even asking about their experience in front of the camera.

"They all got fresh hay and water," Carole promised him.

"Topside seems to have some natural acting ability," Max said. "Even without any makeup or costume, he's passing as a mare!"

Stevie grinned at Max. She should have known that he would have noticed the difference. "He's a pro," Stevie said.

"I should have known you'd come up with some wild scheme," Max said.

"A wild scheme that worked," Stevie reminded him.

"I wish I'd thought of it first," Max confessed. "Nice job."

Stevie sighed, filled with satisfaction. That was a very high compliment from Max. "It's not me who deserves the congratulations," she said. "It's Topside."

"Cut! It's a wrap! Everybody go home!" the director declared.

A few minutes later, Skye arrived to thank the girls. He gave each one of them a hug.

"You were terrific," he said. "You were really good friends to me when I needed them."

"It was fun for us," Stevie said. "We liked teaching you. We'd be glad to do it some more, too."

"I wish," Skye said, removing his riding hat and handing it to a wardrobe assistant. "There's a promotion meeting tonight, followed by a press dinner. Then, we finish the city scenes tomorrow and head back to California the following day. I have a couple of weeks of studio shots, then three days off until I begin my next movie."

"More horseback riding?" Carole asked eagerly.

"No, next time, it's ballet. How are you on pirouettes?"

"We'll learn," Stevie said. "All you have to do is put out the word, and we'll be there. Lisa took a couple of years of it. She can help."

Skye looked at her. "I bet she could," he said, giving Lisa a smile.

"But this time, I don't have to do the performing. See, I just fall in love with a ballerina. Not one jeté for me!"

Lisa felt genuinely disappointed that she and her friends wouldn't have a chance to see Skye again.

"It's been lots of fun," she said. "Really."

"And exciting," Stevie said.

"For me too," he told them. He shook hands with Max and Mrs. Reg and thanked them for all their help. Then, before they could say any more, somebody began calling his name.

"I've got to go," he said. He dashed off toward his trailer.

Lisa had a strange mixture of feelings. She knew that a very exciting adventure was over. She'd probably never see Skye Ransom again. She wasn't going to be his girlfriend, the way she'd dreamed so many nights after reading articles about him. But she didn't want to see that boy she'd read about—not since she'd met the real thing, and gotten to know him. He had a life that was very different from hers, and very different from anything she'd want. She didn't envy him anymore, but she found that, after all was said and done, she liked the real Skye a lot more than she'd ever liked the one in the magazines. It was odd that fate had brought them together once. Would it ever—

"Let's get this horse back to its stall," Max said, gesturing toward Topside.

Lisa abandoned her daydream and turned her attention to Topside.

"YOU SHOULD HAVE seen us switching off lead ropes while they put the horses in the vans!" Stevie told Dorothy excitedly the next morning at the hospital. "We had to get everybody totally confused so no one would know we'd made the switch. But trust me, when you see that movie, it's Topside!"

"I'd know Topside anywhere," Dorothy said. "And it'll be nice to have one more look at him on film."

Carole, standing at the foot of the hospital bed, looked at Dorothy quizzically. "What's that supposed to mean?" she asked.

"Oh, I thought you knew," Dorothy said. "I have to sell Topside."

Stevie looked at Dorothy in astonishment. "But you can't!" she said. "He's too wonderful!"

"He's too wonderful to be useless, you mean," Dorothy said. "That horse was meant to be ridden, to compete. I can't ride him myself and I can't just keep him as a pet. That's not fair to Topside."

There was a long silence in the room. Stevie didn't know what to say. Dorothy was right, but that didn't make Stevie want to know it in her heart. "There must be a way," she said. "I can't stand the idea of some stranger riding that horse."

"I know what you mean, Stevie," Dorothy said. "But the fact is that I've been over this dozens of times in my mind and it always comes up the same way. Topside needs to be ridden and I can't do it. He'll be much better off with a new owner. I'd like to think that he might not spend so much time traveling from show to show. He's good about traveling, but I've always thought he really doesn't like being in vans. Anyway, he does like being in shows and being made to do his best. He's good with inexperienced riders, like Skye, and he's good with experienced ones, too."

Stevie remembered how much she had enjoyed riding Topside, even for that short ride in the park on Staten Island. She'd never been on a horse like that, so full of spirit, yet so controlled.

"Whoever gets him is going to be awfully lucky," Stevie said. For one wild and crazy moment, it occurred to Stevie that she could ask her parents to buy Topside for her. She had to laugh as she imagined their reactions. It was totally hopeless. Stevie reluctantly accepted the fact that her one ride on Topside would be her only ride on Topside.

"I agree." Dorothy said. Then she changed the subject. "So what time does your train leave?" she asked.

"In three and a half hours," Lisa replied. "This has been such a wonderful trip that I can't stand that it's almost over."

"It turned out to be quite different from what we all expected, didn't it?" Dorothy asked.

"Well, we didn't see as much of the horse show as we expected," Carole said. "But we did do a lot of riding and we did a lot of other wonderful things, too."

"Like star in a movie?"

The girls giggled. "The only way Skye could get the director to use us at all was to agree that we'd only be blurs on the screen. Even our parents probably won't recognize us!" Carole told her.

"We could even end up on the cutting-room floor," Lisa said, reminding her friends about the facts of life in Hollywood.

"Listen, you girls don't want to spend your last hours in New York hanging around a hospital room. I know where there's a nice ice cream shop. I'd like to finance a round of sundaes—small pay for taking care of my horse and getting him into the movies!"

The girls would have stayed with Dorothy, but it looked like she was getting tired, so they accepted her offer and, map in hand, returned to the crooked streets of Greenwich Village. Max and Mrs. Reg were expecting them back at Dorothy's in an hour and a half.

"If this place is anything like TD's, we can make it an official Saddle Club meeting," Stevie suggested.

They followed the map and instructions, only got turned around twice, and finally found the shop Dorothy had in mind. It was bright and cheery and had inviting pictures of overwhelming sundaes in the window.

"I feel a Saddle Club meeting coming on," Lisa said.

They were quickly seated in a window booth. As they looked at the menus they couldn't believe the selection. They also couldn't believe the prices!

"Oh, well, it's a fitting way to celebrate our film careers," Carole remarked.

"Sure, by ruining our figures," Stevie agreed.

Lisa leaned back against the soft seat of the booth and closed her eyes.

"Going to sleep?" Stevie teased.

"No, I was just thinking over the trip. It's been like a dream, the whole time . . . even though some of the dream was a nightmare, like Dorothy's accident and the fact that she has to sell Topside. But the rest of it—it's been magical."

"Too bad it can't go on forever," Stevie said.

"Actually," Lisa said, "I don't think I'd want that. In order for there to be magic, there has to be ordinary stuff . . . you know, otherwise, there's nothing magical about the magic. We do have a great secret, you know, about meeting Skye and teaching him to ride and being in the movie."

"We didn't promise we wouldn't tell about being in the movie!" Stevie reminded her. "We just said we wouldn't tell the producers that Skye couldn't ride."

"It doesn't matter anymore," Lisa said. "The movie is almost done and Skye proved he could ride in front of the cameras. So there's no reason we couldn't tell if we wanted to. But who would believe us? People would just say we were making it up. I think it's better if it's a secret."

"Then it's going to be the most special secret I know," Stevie said.

A contented smile came over Lisa's face. "Yes, it is," she agreed.

"Say, on the subject of horses," Carole said, switching directions to her favorite topic, "what would you think about making Dorothy an honorary member of The Saddle Club?"

"I think it's a great idea," Lisa said right away.

"Me too!" Stevie added. "But how do we tell her?"

"I'll make up a certificate," Lisa said eagerly. "Our computer can do anything. As a matter of fact, we ought to have certificates for the full-fledged members, too. And the certificates should be different from one another. I can put sort of curlicues around the edge and I'm sure there's a horse graphic. There are a bunch of different type styles. I wonder if I can make the letters go in a circle . . . and if I get really busy with this, then maybe I won't be as likely to tell our secret to everyone on the planet!"

The waitress arrived then to take their orders. Lisa and Carole ordered vanilla ice cream with hot fudge and caramel, respectively. Then they waited, curious to see what Stevie would do. At TD's she always ordered truly outrageous sundaes. They suspected she did it to keep them from taking tastes of her sundae.

"Is it French vanilla?" Stevie asked.

"Yes," the waitress said patiently.

"And the fudge swirl is made with Swiss chocolate?"

"Yes," the woman said, twirling a lock of hair with her pencil. She looked like she'd answered these questions before.

"Okay, then, I'll have bubble-gum ice cream with butterscotch sauce."

"Okay," the woman said, jotting down Stevie's order. She turned slowly, and then fled.

"I just wanted to see how she would react," Stevie said. "New Yorkers have probably seen it all, but I thought maybe I could get to her."

"You got to her, all right," Lisa said. She pointed to where their waitress stood, surrounded by other waitresses and waiters. They were staring at the order pad and then glancing curiously at Stevie. "Now the question is, will you actually be able to eat that mess?"

She ate every bite. And when the waitress asked her to sign the check, just to prove that somebody had actually eaten it, Stevie agreed immediately.

She signed it "Princess Di."

*   *   *

"I CAN'T BELIEVE this, Lisa," Max said. "You arrived in this city with four suitcases, and you're going home with five!" He hefted two of them down the stairs at Dorothy's house to put them with the rest of the luggage. It was time to go.

"Well, Max, you know what they say about this being a great place to shop! Look at the T-shirts we got today!" Each girl wore a shirt that read "Oi luv Noo Yawk!"

Max smiled indulgently. "Okay, all right." He shook his head, though. The girls hid their giggles. Lisa actually still only had four suitcases. They'd just told Max Stevie's was hers, too, to get a rise out of him. It had worked.

There was a car waiting for them at the door. It took them a few minutes to load everything in. Then they turned to thank Jean DeSoto.

It was hard to say thank-you to her. The trip had been so special that Lisa didn't know how to tell her. And, at the same time, the DeSotos had a difficult time ahead with Dorothy's recovery. Lisa felt awkward.

Mrs. DeSoto made it easy for her and the other girls. She held out her arms and hugged them all at once.

"You come back, now," Mrs. DeSoto said. "We can use a little excitement from time to time!"

The girls grinned and hugged her back.

"Come on, the car's ready to go," Mrs. Reg said from the back seat. The girls piled into the car with Mrs. Reg and Max and they were off.

13

THE TRAIN STATION wasn't far, and Max, in his usual superorganized manner, had allowed plenty of time.

Carole looked out of the window of the car and gazed at the city streets as they passed. She saw the place where they'd first seen Skye's movie company, in the park. She saw the place where Lisa had gotten her hair cut. There was the ice cream parlor, the store where they'd bought their T-shirts. Then she spotted the entrance to the subway they'd taken to the Plaza. It seemed everywhere she looked there were hundreds of great memories.

Soon, she knew, they'd be passing Madison Square Garden, where the horse show was still taking place. But Dorothy wasn't part of it—and she never would be again. Carole shook her head, trying to loosen the thought. Dorothy wouldn't want her to dwell on it, either.

They stopped at a light and she watched three girls jump rope in a little park. She hoped those girls had as much fun together as she did with Stevie and Lisa. Their friendship was the most important thing in the world to her—next to horseback riding.

Beyond the little girls, she saw a whole row of trailers parked.

"Look at that," she said. "Looks like the kind they take on a movie location!"

Stevie, sitting in the middle, looked out the window over Carole. "Sure does," she said. "Do you suppose . . . ?"

"Take a left, driver," Lisa said authoritatively.

Before Max or Mrs. Reg could object, the driver swung to the left and drove along a side street, approaching the vans.

"It sure looks like it," Lisa said, excitement rising in her voice.

"Could it be?" Carole said.

"Of course it is!" Lisa said. "Look at all the girls the police are holding behind the lines there. It's got to be! Only Skye Ransom could get a crowd like that!"

The car pulled up to the curb.

"Can we see?" Stevie asked. Max looked at his watch and shrugged his shoulders. "Ten minutes can't hurt," he said. That was all the girls needed. They were out of the car in a flash.

"This way," Stevie said, leading them to where she could see the lights set up.

They got within about fifty yards of the location set when a policeman tried to shoo them behind the barricade.

"But Officer," Stevie explained, using her most convincing voice. "Skye Ransom's a friend of ours. We just want to say hello."

"And the mayor's a friend of mine," the officer said calmly, "and he just wants me to keep all you teenage girls behind these lines, see?"

Before they knew what was happening, they were in the midst of a very large, excited crowd of girls their own age. Every single one of them just wanted a look at Skye Ransom.

"We met him, you know," Stevie said to the girl standing next to her.

"Yeah, sure," the girl said. She didn't sound as if she believed Stevie.

"And we went riding with him," Lisa told her, trying to be convincing.

"Riding? That's all? I went dancing with him last night, and the night before. Miriam," she said, turning to her friend, "what was your dream?"

"A cruise," the girl said. "We took a cruise together. And when a wave rocked the ship, he kept me from being swept overboard!"

"Well, when he fell off his horse, I helped him," Lisa told the girls.

They looked at her with distaste. "Skye would *never* fall off a horse," Miriam said. "He's a very good rider. I read all about it in *Teen Month*."

Lisa, Stevie, and Carole looked at one another and laughed. They'd been absolutely right in the first place. Nobody was going to believe them.

"I think we'd better go," Lisa said sensibly. "Standing behind this barrier isn't going to get us anyplace."

The girls ducked under the barrier and returned to the car.

They climbed into the rear seat and the driver took them to Pennsylvania Station.

It wasn't until they were on the train and Max had stowed all of their bags that they realized Max didn't have his luggage.

"Do you have time to go get your suitcase before the train goes?" Carole asked with concern.

"Nope," Max said lightly. "So I guess I'll just have to stay in New York another couple of days."

"Another couple of days!" Stevie said. "How long will it take you to get the suitcase?"

"Oh, that'll only take me a few minutes. What's going to take me a little longer is filing all the papers and hiring a van and car to bring Topside home to Willow Creek."

"Well, sure, of course," Stevie said. "That kind of thing does take time. I mean, everybody knows about filing papers. And vans can be—" She stopped in mid-sentence because Max's words had just registered.

"You mean?"

Max nodded.

132

"Really?" Carole asked.

Max nodded again.

"For *us?*" Lisa asked.

"Who else?" he said. "I couldn't let Dorothy sell a wonderful horse like that to just anybody. And, knowing how good Topside is—both with new riders like Skye Ransom and experienced ones like Dorothy— well, I thought he'd be the best horse I could get to train my next few championship riders."

Stevie couldn't help herself. She leapt up out of her seat on the train to give Max a bear hug.

Carole and Lisa shrieked with joy and excitement.

"I'm glad I've got your approval," Max said. "Now settle down and take care of my mother on the trip home. I'll be along by the middle of the week. You girls have class on Wednesday, right? Well, you can spend the entire trip home arguing about who gets to ride Topside first. Mother, I recommend you take that seat across the aisle and let these three sit together. They're going to get rowdy and you won't want people to think you're with them," he teased.

The train's whistle blew. Max dashed for the exit and made it back onto the platform right before the train started moving. The girls and Mrs. Reg waved out the window to him.

Mrs. Reg settled into the seat across the aisle and pulled a magazine out of her handbag.

"Alphabetical, that's the fair way," Carole said. "So, since Carole comes before Lisa and Stevie—"

"Yeah, but Atwood comes before Hanson and Lake," Lisa reminded her.

"By height," Stevie said. "The tallest should go first!"

"No, the oldest!" Lisa countered.

"No, the best rider!" Carole said.

"I've got it," Stevie announced, smiling sweetly. "The *nicest* goes first."

"Hmm," Carole said thoughtfully, breaking off the friendly argument temporarily. "I've been thinking about leaving all the fun and excitement of New York and how nice it will be to get back to dull old Willow Creek where nothing exciting ever happens."

"How can you say that?" Lisa asked, truly astonished.

Carole smiled wryly. "But then I thought about it some more, and I realized that it doesn't much matter where we are, because wherever there's The Saddle Club, there's always *something* exciting going on!"

Lisa and Stevie nodded. It was true. It was great to be at the horse show and meet Skye Ransom, but The Saddle Club was what really mattered.

"I've got it!" Lisa announced, returning to their earlier subject. "Highest grades rides him first!"

"Highest military rank achieved by a father!"

"Most brothers!"

"Fewest brothers!"

"Most sisters!"

"We don't have any sisters!" they yelled in unison.

By the time they'd reached Philadelphia, the girls were laughing too hard to care who rode Topside first—as long as they all got turns.

ABOUT THE AUTHOR

BONNIE BRYANT is the author of more than thirty books for young readers, including the best-selling novelizations of *The Karate Kid* movies. The Saddle Club books are her first for Bantam-Skylark. She wrote her first book six years ago and has been busy at her word processor ever since. (For her first three years as an author, Ms. Bryant was also working in the office of a publishing company. In 1986, she left her job to write full-time.)

Whenever she can, Ms. Bryant goes horseback riding in her hometown, New York City. She's had many riding experiences in the city's Central Park that have found their way into her Saddle Club books—and lots which haven't!

The author has two sons, and they all live together in an apartment in Greenwich Village that is just too small for a horse.

Saddle up for great reading with

T·H·E
SADDLE CLUB

A blue-ribbon series by Bonnie Bryant

Stevie, Carole and Lisa are all very different, but they *love* horses! The three girls are best friends at Pine Hollow Stables, where they ride and care for all kinds of horses. Come to Pine Hollow and get ready for all the fun and adventure that comes with being 13!

Don't miss this terrific 10-book series. Collect them all!

☐ 15594 HORSE CRAZY #1 .... $2.75
☐ 15611 HORSE SHY #2 .... $2.75
☐ 15626 HORSE SENSE #3 .... $2.75
☐ 15637 HORSE POWER #4 .... $2.75
☐ 15703 TRAIL MATES #5 .... $2.75
☐ 15728 DUDE RANCH #6 .... $2.75
☐ 15754 HORSE PLAY #7 .... $2.75
☐ 15769 HORSE SHOW #8 .... $2.75

Watch for other SADDLE CLUB books all year. More great reading—and riding to come!

Buy them at your local bookstore or use this handy page for ordering.